Step On…over to the dark, passionate side of life. Or is that death?

Dark Side of the Moon – Recovering from a near fatal injury, vampire Harley Scott just wants some peace, quiet and a long night filled with darkness. The wilds of icy Canada sounds like the best place to make that happen – if he can make it past blizzards, werewolves, and a death squad of fellow vampires on his trail.

Soul Desire – Can passion reach past the grave? Does the urge for love or justice live beyond the physical existence? Mason Everett gets the unfortunate chance to find out.

Shadows in Time – Trying to avoid ruin and disgrace, young, naive Neal Clifton, wealthy heir to a sizable Boston family fortune faces the illicit and dangerous complication of his first affair with man – a scheming, unscrupulous man with influence and power that reaches beyond the grave. Neal vows to never give into his own unnatural desires again, but finds his only hope for escape in the hands (and arms) of stoic silversmith, Peter Wade.

Step On

Laura Baumbach

Copyright 2016 by Laura Baumbach

Published by
MLR Press, LLC
3052 Gaines Waterport Rd.
Albion, NY 14411

Visit ManLoveRomance Press, LLC on the Internet:
www.mlrpress.com

Cover Art by Winterheart Design
Editing by Judith David and Kris Jacen

Print format: ISBN# 978-1-94477-022-8
ebook format also available

Issued 2016

Table of Contents

Dark Side of the Moon

The thrum of the diesel truck wound down to a low hum then sighed into silence. Only the fierce whine of the winds blowing around the high cab filled the night air. It was cold and bitter and the last thing Harley Scott wanted to do was uncurl from his warm leather seat nesting spot against the thick passenger door.

He shouldn't be bothered by the cold, or the long hours riding across the frozen Canadian territories in a loud, vibrating semi, but little things bothered him lately. Lately, as in since he got shot in the head a month ago. What was supposed to be an ordinary one night stand for sex and a snack turned out bad. It was just going to be a few hours with a new john who had bought Harley's willing body for the night. Unfortunately, the sadistic john enjoyed himself so much, he decided he wanted to act out his own snuff film with Harley as the snuffee.

Harley had shrugged it off at first as what you get when you're into blood sports. What's a little strangulation to a vampire? He didn't need to breathe. But he hadn't expected the gun. He did need all his brain cells intact.

Harley had suffered life-altering, lasting effects from the head wound, but at least he still existed. The john had actually suffered a heart attack and died. Must have had something to do with Harley regaining consciousness after the bullet penetrated his brain and sitting up to swear and curse out his shooter. Or it could have been the fact that he had done it in full vampire mode with fangs extended, eyes glowing and the primal animal need for restorative blood taking hold of the moment.

Except that the man's blood, no matter how much Harley had taken, had not restored him. Not by much. Nothing had since then, either, and word of his injury had spread throughout the tightly monitored vampire community he had been taken into at his conversion. The elders now labeled him defective and crippled, unfit for continued existence.

They never had been happy that he continued being a hustler and a whore after being made into a vampire. He'd given up on his dream of a regular life and a family when he became a night creature. His decision to stay in his old hustler's lifestyle was an element that gave him a sense of security and comfort amid the many changes he was forced to endure. He found it an easy way to make money and feed without detection. The elders found it degrading and unnecessary and not to be tolerated, especially from a 'defective' vampire.

Which was why Harley was on the run, trying oh so hard to elude the two Eliminators on his tail.

Which was also why he was sitting in the cab of a semi in a small and garishly lit truck stop on the way to somewhere isolated and unattractive in a dark, frozen wilderness. Somewhere the Eliminators wouldn't look.

Even Harley didn't have any idea where he was just now.

One glance at the overweight, pockmarked trucker beside him and Harley quickly averted his glance to the wide windshield and checked out the sky. It looked like dawn would be approaching in the next hour or so. He couldn't rely on his senses to tell him when morning was nearing anymore. It was all a crapshoot now. Being in a strange place, traveling nearer and nearer to the territories where three months were in almost total darkness made it even harder to judge sunrise.

But Harley knew one blowjob, even with the quick snack from the sweaty man's femoral artery, was all he was willing to give the man. The trucker smelled of old cigars and cheap whiskey, and his blood was thick with plaque and fat— as unappetizing as the man's odor.

Slipping into his completely inadequate leather biker's jacket, Harley cracked the heavy door open and slid to the ground before the trucker could comment or protest. He nodded at the guy as he pulled the small duffel bag off the cab floor and out of the truck. It didn't hold much.

"Thanks for the ride, Sam. It's been a pleasure." Harley knew his voice sounded sincere. He'd had decades to practice. Whether the john had been any good or not, it paid to make them think they had been. It increased the tip sometimes and made for repeat business. In this case, Harley hoped he never saw the sweaty, bloated man again.

He nodded toward the brightly-lit cafe a few hundred feet away. "Any idea where we are?"

The harshly blowing wind whipped up and nearly tore

the door out of his hands. "Damn it!" Harley tugged the door closer to his body to block the chill and waited for Sam to say something so he could move out of the weather and into the building.

He really wanted to be somewhere safer, but right now just dark and warm would do. The vampires following him might be close, but the sun was even closer. In his present physical condition, even the weak rays that cut through this thick, swirling snow would do irreparable harm.

"You coming in?"

Sam eyed the cheery cafe and then shrugged. "Nah. I usually just sleep at this stop. The regulars here are too talkative for me. I like peace and quiet."

Since all Sam had done since Harley got into the truck cab was talk, the declaration surprised him, but he didn't waste much time thinking about it. It was too cold and he was too tired to care. "Where did you say we are?"

"You're just outside of Ross River. I'm heading west to hook up with the Interstate 2 then hitting Dawson. Got a load to deliver and one to pick up. You're welcome to make the trip." Sam leered in what Harley knew the man thought was a seductive grin. The smile showed every one of the man's tobacco-stained teeth and twisted his two-day chin stubble into a grizzled, knotted nest. "The toll for riders ain't that high, if you get my drift." The trucker winked and Harley felt his stomach roll.

He could avoid having sex with the man, but even the taste of Sam's blood wasn't something he wanted to repeat. He just wanted to be far away from everyone right now. He gnawed on one of his own knuckles until it bled, then sucked on the torn flesh and thin blood, hoping to make the nausea and faint hunger go away.

"Thanks anyway, but I think maybe I'll hang around here for a bit and see if anyone is headed east. Thanks for the ride this far." A gust of wind shoved him bodily to one side. Harley used it as an excuse to close the truck door, blocking out the sight of the man's disappointed face.

Bent low to keep the strong gales from lifting his slim frame right off the ice-packed surface under his feet, Harley shivered under the unlined leather of his jacket. He jammed his fists into its pockets and trudged rapidly over the two hundred feet between him and the protection of the little cafe.

He didn't know if Sam was following him and didn't care. He just wanted out of the cold. He looked forward to the continual darkness the extreme territories had to offer him now, but the bitter cold here affected him more than he thought possible.

Two new arrivals to the stop descended from their trucks as he passed by their still running cabs. He nodded and sized each man up to be sure neither of the two vampires on his trail had slipped up on him. He couldn't sense the presence of his own kind like he should be able to, but he could still pick out a scent close up.

Both of these big, brawny men were human. A single sniff told him that once they were beside him. One smelled earthy, faintly like pine and campfire smoke, and an undefined but strong scent that teased at the edges of Harley's memory. In the end it eluded him, and he shook his head to clear it, unconcerned. These were flesh and blood creatures with heartbeats, not vampires in disguise. The unnamed scent didn't matter. He was safe, for the moment, from his executioners.

The other man reeked of Italian seasonings, garlic in particular. Harley smiled when he recognized the once dreaded scent and he inhaled deeply. Before his head wound, the smell would have made him cringe. Now it almost made his mouth water. One more sign his life was going back to hell in a hand basket.

After over thirty years as a vampire, it was brutal to have to revert to a partially humanized state, however temporary he hoped it was. He hadn't realized how good he'd had it as a vampire. He'd never been bothered by extreme temperatures, petty illness or physical defects. Now he was cold, weak and if he was being truthful with himself, terrified. Eliminators weren't known for the humane way they rid the world of 'defective' vampires — what they now considered him to be.

Just thinking of the stories he'd heard about the 'monster killers' made the nausea boil up in his gut again. He liked the eyes in his head. They were nice, hazel eyes, slightly exotic looking with their almost-almond shape and oddly crystallized threads of green, blue, gray and black. One of his best seductive features, he'd been told. He wanted them left right where they were. His head looked best on his shoulders, too. Decapitation, evisceration, enucleation, and amputation were all such ugly words, words the Eliminators worked hard to create new, more horrendous definitions for.

Hurrying, the leather soles of his boots made him lose his footing twice on the slick blacktop. He reached for the door handle just as the earth-tainted trucker let go of it. The man stopped, sniffed, turned back and then held the door open for Harley.

"You're gonna freeze your assets off, boy. That little bitty jacket ain't made for this neck of the woods." The man looked to be in his forties, broad shouldered, with a fringe of washed-out honey-blond hair under a fur hat with earflaps. His bulk was wrapped in layers of clothing beneath a heavy brown canvas coat. Despite the suggestiveness of his comment, the look on the man's reddened face was part disbelief and part amusement, with a touch of fatherly sternness.

"I can take it." Harley smiled back, radiating what he knew was a confident gleam in his eye. The gleam was destroyed when a violent shiver visibly shook his entire body. He had enough grace to look sheepish. "But I don't have to like it."

"Better get on in here and warm up then. Take a stool at the counter in the middle. That'll sit you right by one of the heating vents." The trucker herded Harley through the vestibule into the main diner, a concerned hand on Harley's hunched shoulder.

"Name's Abe, by the way." Abe grabbed Harley's hand and vigorously shook it.

"Ah, yeah." Harley wiped the sweat from the man's palm onto his jeans, then wrapped his arms around his chest to contain another shiver, this one less violent but still evident. He hoped Abe wouldn't notice he didn't return the courtesy of giving his own name. "Nice to meet you."

They walked over a strip of bright yellow symbols on the floor and another shiver shook Harley's lean frame, making him pause. A sudden stabbing pain in his head made the healing bullet wound burn. The room wavered for a moment, but Harley shook off the accompanying wave of dizziness. Under Abe's watchful eye, he moved farther into the cafe to sit down.

"Damn, son, you are pale." Abe drew in a deep breath and sniffed, wrinkling his nose like it itched. "I've seen road kill looked better than you."

Abe shoved Harley in the direction of the swivel-mounted stools in front of a gray laminated counter top where half a dozen patrons sat in various stages of drinking and eating.

Abe slipped out of his jacket and called out to a plump woman dressed in a pink fleece jogging suit. She wore a big smile and too much blue eye shadow. "Betty, we got a young one here that needs some looking after. Get him some of your good home cookin' before he drops over in a dead faint from the chills."

Smiling despite himself at the 'dead' comment, Harley nodded his thanks as Betty instantly gravitated toward them.

"Got just the thing for him, Abe, honey. Show the boy where to sit." Betty flashed Harley a bright smile that dimmed a bit as she really looked at him. "Boy's white as a ghost."

Betty unexpectedly reached out and patted Harley's cold cheek, then huffed in apparent disapproval. She turned on her heel and hustled toward the kitchen area, calling over her shoulder to no one in particular. "Somebody sit him down before he falls down while I find him something to warm his insides."

Abe pointed a beefy, callused finger at an empty stool two seats away. "You heard the woman, son, sit down. Get yourself some hot coffee and a bowl of Betty's biscuits and gravy. She'll put you to rights." Abe turned his attention to greeting two of the men already seated at the counter, but Harley noticed the man kept a watchful eye on him until he took his stool.

Once he sat down, Harley made sure that, when he swiveled the stool to his left, he had a good view of the front door. According to the aged and yellowed signs on the far wall, the bathrooms were conveniently located to his right. Bathrooms were usually by back doors and sometimes had windows. Escape routes were always foremost in his mind.

His sense of time had also been disrupted by the bullet, but he knew the dawn had to be very close now. If no truckers left the diner soon that he could hitch a ride with, he might have to spend the day sleeping in one of the bathroom stalls to stay out of sight and out of the direct light.

Harley gazed out the large, insulated picture window behind him and watched the dancing snow shift and pirouette against the glass, the shriek of the wind louder and more foreboding than only a few minutes ago. It made his bones ache, the mournful screams sending a tingle of unease down his spine. What he wouldn't give to be in a quiet, dark room alone, safe, warm and unbothered.

As he turned his back on the darkness and snow, a cup of steaming coffee and a large bowl of chicken soup slid under his nose. Betty had returned.

"This'll help some. Warm you up and put some color and heat back in those cold cheeks of yours, sweetie." Betty patted his hand, fingers rubbing over the slowly healing scars from his own teeth. "Your hands are all cut up, darlin'." She added, "Stop biting your nails!" Even though it was obviously not his problem. She patted his hands again, an understanding look in her eye. "You want a second helpin' on the soup, you just holler. On the house." With a wink and another pat, she was off to refill coffee cups and banter with her new arrivals.

Harley was surprised to realize he liked her. When she leaned in close, she smelled like lemons and cedar to him. He'd liked lemon drops when he was human. They tasted tart but pleasing. The scent suited Betty.

The hunger stirred slightly in him and he couldn't help wonder what her blood tasted like but, before he could embrace the urge, the desire wafted away leaving him hollow and tired again. He didn't even have to bite his fingers to quell it this time.

God, he wanted to feel better. His appetite had all but disappeared and without nourishment he'd never heal. The only time he had the urge to even snack now was during sex and that was proving to be an opportunity that happened more and more rarely these days. He just didn't have the energy for it.

Sighing, Harley pretended to sip at the soup while he let the warmth of its fragrant steam waft up into his face and invade his nose and lungs. Cold hands wrapped around the hot ceramic coffee mug, he closed his eyes and let his thoughts drift like the vapor rising off the hot food. It was comfortable and homey here. It gave him the illusion of being safe.

He stirred only once, jumping slightly when Abe slapped his back and gruffly commanded, "Eat up, son, won't do you any good in the bowl." The big man passed behind him on his way to the bathroom.

Harley nodded but remained motionless, mind drifting to more pleasant times as he basked in the warm air blasting out of the heating vent near him.

He didn't know how long he had been daydreaming again, but he started for a second time at the sound of the diner door snapping open. A blast of cold air fought for entrance into the toasty warm room and out of the corner of his eye he saw something that turned his pleasant daydream to dust.

With his sluggish post-injury reactions further hindered by lack of sleep and inadequate nourishment, Harley wasn't sure if he had moved fast enough. Once in the protection of the tiny alcove leading to the bathrooms, he peeked at the other vampire. Two more truckers had entered along with the Eliminator, partially blocking his view. Harley hoped they had blocked him from the assassin's view as well, but he didn't wait around to find out. His lingering scent, diseased and distinct to his own kind, would be enough to confirm his presence within seconds.

Banking on the building being old enough to have a window in the bathrooms, he tore into the men's room and shut the door, leaning his weight against it, forehead resting on the solid steel. He tried to calm his buzzing, confused senses but the effort seemed pointless. He'd had few defenses against these assassins when he had been strong and healthy. Now, weak, without most of his vampire abilities and alone, he didn't stand a chance. His only defense was to run, but dawn was already on the horizon.

A cold draft of air struck the back of his neck, telling Harley that the room did indeed have a window. A window someone else must have just recently used. Used to come into the bathroom. Used to be ready and waiting for him when he tried the same thing. Suddenly the vampire on the other side of the door wasn't as important as the one on this side.

Scrabbling vainly for the door handle, Harley was grabbed by the scruff of his neck and thrown up against the wall beside the door, back slamming hard into the rough paneled wall. The short leather jacket, scrunched high up his back by the attack, allowed slivers of pine from the wall to gouge his skin. One slid deep between his shoulder blades. A scarred face, more animal than human, shoved up close to his own and the glow of fevered yellow eyes bore into his.

The vampire was tall and angular, sharp-boned, and thin, but unbridled power and strength radiated off him in waves. Strong and bony, the vampire's hands were out of Harley's view, one crushed against Harley's throat and the other with a strangle hold on Harley's balls. The sneer on his lips couldn't be described as anything short of malicious.

"What's the hurry, rentboy?" The voice was unexpectedly deep and sensual. "It's said you do some of your best work in public bathrooms."

The hold on his balls tightened. Harley grimaced and gasped, fingers working frantically to loosen the deadly grip on his throat. He couldn't answer, even if he'd wanted to. He didn't need to breathe, but he couldn't talk without breathing.

The vampire leaned in closer and licked up Harley's jaw to his hair line, the thick muscle immediately finding the small, healed scar from the bullet wound and pressing on it.

The tiny, still-knitting bone fragments under Harley's scalp shifted minutely. Harley thrashed and clawed at the vampire's hands, the resulting flash of pain and nausea almost more than he could stand.

The sudden jiggle of change and a belt buckle was drowned out by the flushing of a toilet that startled both of them. Abe lumbered out of one of the stalls and strode toward them, gaze locking on the Eliminator's grip on Harley's neck.

"What the hell's going on here?"

The vampire swiftly drew back, releasing Harley, but not before Abe's gaze dropped to see the hold the vampire had on Harley's crotch.

The trucker strode brazenly up to Harley's side and shoved his bulk between the two, forcing the Eliminator to back off a few steps more. Despite Abe's obvious physical strength for a human, Harley knew the only thing keeping the man alive right now was the Eliminator's dislike of a complication like one of involving a human in their work.

"This asshole giving you trouble, son?" Abe ran a harsh glare over the tall vampire's now empty, grasping hands and then pointedly brought his gaze up to the creature's sneering face. He spared Harley a quick glance. "You hurt?"

Tired of being treated like he was a weakling and a failure, Harley threw a disdainful glare back at Abe. "Not your concern. Just a misunderstanding. I can handle it."

A grunt of displeasure hissed out of the tall vampire. "Listen to him, mister. Butt out." He spit on the floor, giving both men a disgusted glare. "He's right, he likes to be handled. Don't you, boy?"

Ignoring Harley's biting dismissal, Abe bristled and moved forward. The Eliminator visibly tensed, a snarl on his thin, colorless lips.

Harley readied himself for another attack, one where both he and Abe came out the losers. No human could withstand this kind of vampire attack and Harley couldn't defend himself, let alone Abe. Not that he was inclined to protect a human, but all the same, it would be a bloodbath.

The tall vampire snarled, and took a step closer so he was chest to chest with the brawnier trucker, eager anticipation on his face.

As if on cue, the door burst open and the two truckers who had arrived after Harley and Abe, barreled into the room. They both pulled up short, eyeing the standoff.

"Hell now, what's the problem in here, Abe?" The smaller of the two new arrivals stood beside Abe, jabbing one knobby fist into his open palm as he stared at the tall, dark stranger facing off with his friend.

Not wanting things to escalate, Harley took advantage of the open door and the wall of aggressive flesh between himself and his assassin and fled the room. But once out in the main diner, he pulled up short again.

The first rays of dawn filtered through the wide glass front of the diner, a gray, hazy light that made Harley sweat and his stomach roll with terror. But it wasn't nearly as frightening as the man that stood by the front door just to the far side of the yellow symbols decorating the floor. One dressed identically to the vampire Harley had just left behind in the men's room. From the black down parka to the unforgiving sneer, he was obviously one of a pair.

This encounter was the first time Harley had seen the Eliminators in person. He'd been running from rumors and menacing shadows since the first whispered tip-offs that they were after him filtered through the seedy bloodsport circles he had inhabited as a pay-for-play sex toy.

A few people had told him about his coming fate at the hand of the Eliminators, but no one, not even vampires he had know for thirty years, had stood up for him or offered to help him. No one until these humans, these strangers. He consoled himself with the certain knowledge that they wouldn't have done so either if they knew what he really was—a blood-drinking member of the elite undead that walked among them.

In the last thirty years Harley hadn't killed anyone since the very first hunger consumed him. He'd come close during the following few weeks of learning to control the urge to take more than he needed, but he'd always believed in live and let live, even after the change.

Besides, killing every man who paid to sleep with you was a poor way to build a clientele. Snacking and sipping on several johns a night was plenty and the sex was better that way too.

Harley was physically slight and his blood desire was small compared to some of his breed. Since his head wound, his urges had dwindled to next to nothing. His body demanded more, but his stomach couldn't oblige.

Right now his gut felt like it was turning inside out.

He stood paralyzed, reluctant to step into the growing pre-dawn light and draw a step closer to the same fate that he had just slipped away from. He suddenly, surprisingly, missed Abe's solid presence.

Undoubtedly alerted by the vampire ability to sense their own, the new stranger instantly locked his gaze onto Harley. He just stood by the doorway, confidently waiting for Harley to come to him.

Harley could tell by the way the vampire flared his nostrils that he had picked out Harley's scent and found it unappealing. It only took a second for the gleam of triumph to light up the Eliminator's eyes. This assassin actually pursed his lips to keep a twisted smile from showing but failed. It chilled Harley more than the other killer's cruel sneers had.

There was a sudden warmth near him and Harley started to see Abe at his side. Harley glanced behind to see the two other truckers amble out of the men's room and retake their seats at the counter. Abe threw an arm across Harley's shoulders and shoved him gently forward, his larger body blocking the sun from Harley as they walked.

"I'm heading west toward Whitehorse." Abe's deep voice boomed over the rattle of plates and the chatter of the other diners. "Got room in the cab for one more, if you need a ride."

Harley watched the smile melt away from the vampire's face and he felt like a drowning man thrown a rope from shore. He opened his mouth to answer, but surprised himself when nothing came out but a shaky breath.

"Leaving in about fifteen seconds so make up your mind damn quick, son." This time Abe's voice was firm and insistent, like a father making a suggestion to a child, but actually expecting it to be taken as the order it really was.

"Yeah. Okay." Harley licked his lips, unable to break

his gaze away from the doorway killer's vengeful, burning stare. "I could go west."

The gray sunlight slid further into the room and Harley felt a surge of panic compete with dread. Both wanted to be the cause of the headache threatening to crush through his head. The pressure the other vamp had applied to his healing, still fragile skull had been almost enough to drop him to his knees earlier. Its lingering affects made him dizzy and his reactions slow. "For a little while. West would work."

"Great. Let's go." Abe pushed Harley forward toward the end of the counter where Betty stood with a worn, yellow parka in her arms.

"You're not dressed for this part of the country, child. Take this." She held out the coat to Harley, then fussed and circled him until she had worked the too-big coat up his arms and over his shoulders, the leather biker jacket underneath. The coat still had room left in it.

She zipped up the first few inches of the jacket. "My youngest left this behind when he went off on his own. Too small for him now. It's been hanging on a peg by the back door for a year. Someone might as well get some use out of it." She thrust a lidded Styrofoam cup into his hand and he smelled chicken soup.

Speechless, Harley could only stare at her and wonder what had caused the act of generosity. He liked her scent, but he'd barely spoken to her. He managed a jerky nod of thanks, then wished he'd done better when that small gesture brought a huge smile to her weathered face.

"You'll find someplace to warm up soon." Betty patted his cheek, then her fingers traveled upward to brush gently over the hidden bullet wound under his dark bangs. Harley couldn't help but flinch at the unexpected sharp pain her light touch caused.

Betty jerked her hand away and tsked, "Still too cold. Be careful, you hear?"

Abe didn't wait for Harley to find his voice. Coat back on and headgear in place to protect his balding head and exposed ears, he pushed Harley past the frustrated vampire at the door and straight out into the pale dawn. A wave of dizziness washed over Harley as he went out the door, but he kept moving.

The vampire followed them out the door.

Two feet from the exit, the clouds broke and sunlight bathed the whole area. Harley heard a hiss of displeasure from behind him that made him move faster into the light. Disintegrating in sunlight was still better than decapitation any day. Quicker, anyway.

Harley yanked the parka over his head, rolled his fists in the fabric and out of the threatening beams of light. He raced to the purring rig Abe pointed at, hoping he didn't leave a trail of smoke in his wake.

Huddled in the shadow of the rig, he dove into the cab as soon as Abe opened the door and hunched down in the seat, coat still over his head. Sliding up until his eyes were level with the dashboard, he could just barely see into the diner window as Abe pulled out of the parking lot. He made out a pair of dark shapes standing off to one side in the shadows of the main diner, side by side. He was glad he couldn't see their faces. He had enough nightmares as it was.

Abe pulled the truck back onto the highway and geared up to running speed before turning his attention to Harley.

By now, Harley was nearly on the floor, curled in a ball and buried under the baggy parka, in an attempt to avoid the beams of sunlight coming through the side window.

"Why don't you crawl into the back cab, son? There's a nice sized bunk and lots of blankets." Abe jerked a thumb over his shoulder at the opening that led to the sleeper compartment. "You look like you could use a few hours in the rack."

Eyes darting between the sleeper and Abe's neutral expression, Harley let past experiences and exhaustion rule his tongue. "Alone?"

Abe's expression hardened. "Listen, son, you don't have anything I want."

"Why are you doing this? You don't know me at all."

"Where I come from, we stick together; take care of them that need caring for. Whether you admit it or not, son, you could use a little being cared for." Abe's voice was quiet and oddly sad. "Get some sleep. Go on. Get." He made an abrupt shooing motion.

Not having to be told twice, Harley dove for the bunk in an uncoordinated scramble that left him dizzy and nauseated, but comfortably secluded in the sleeper's windowless nook. Without another word, he closed the curtain, shutting out the sunlight and the disgruntled look on the man's face.

He couldn't believe these people. These human strangers had stood up for him, even protected him at the diner, without wanting something in return. Life, or living death, wasn't like that. At least, not the existence he'd been leading.

Shoving a scarred knuckle into his mouth, he bit down and tasted the blood, more out of habit now than real desire. Lulled by the rhythm of the road and the warmth of the blankets and bed, Harley fell asleep with a vague sense of contentment and security he couldn't understand. He didn't think he liked it.

§ § §

When he woke, Harley was relieved the sun had disappeared and the truck was still moving. A faint decrease in their speed had awakened him, and he watched Abe gear down his engine speed as they approached the outskirts of a town. Reluctantly, Harley slipped out from under the warm blankets to see where he had ended up.

After Abe announced what direction they were headed in, the trailing vampires wouldn't be far behind them. That was once they were freed by the fading of the short-lived daylight. He was pretty sure their mood hadn't been improved by the events in the diner. He was also sure he hadn't eluded them by much. Harley would have to move quickly once the rig stopped if he planned on disappearing among whatever this new huddle of humanity had to offer him.

He slid wordlessly into the passenger seat again; grateful Abe kept his greeting to a nod and a pleased-sounding grunt.

The sliver of wood from the bathroom wall burned between his shoulder blades, unreachable by himself. His head still ached, and the smell of Abe's warm skin awakened his appetite. Harley gnawed at the side of one finger until it started to bleed. Of late, that had been enough to appease the hunger.

"This here is Kai. It's little, but not too little. You should be able to find a place to stay on the north end that won't cost you a lot. Try a place called 'Sugar's'. It's clean." Abe looked him over silently for a moment before asking, "Need some cash?"

There was nothing suggestive or provocative about the question, just a note of concern that made Harley's hackles rise. "Not staying long." He sucked on the thin trickle of blood from his finger, trying to make it look like a nervous habit and not a distraction meant to keep him from piercing Abe's jugular for a long drink.

"You worried about those two we left back there at Betty's?" Abe smirked.

"Not exactly." Feeling defensive, Harley was quick to point out it was the man's fault he had to keep running. "They heard what you said about going west. They'll be following us."

Abe's smirk widened. "Figured as much." He pointed

up, gesturing toward the clear night sky full of stars. "That's why you're so far north they'll need a whole season to find you. Even then it'd take a pack of bloodhounds to sniff you out, son. You might as well be on the dark side of the moon."

Stunned, it took Harley a moment before he could respond. "You lied about where you were headed?" He frowned, suddenly unhappy with all the effort this stranger was making on his behalf. He didn't need looking after. "For me? Why?"

"Don't hurt a man none to be generous when it doesn't cost him anything. I was headed this way." Abe brought the truck to a smooth rolling stop at a momentarily deserted intersection. Nodding at the line of lights down the main street, he gave Harley an encouraging wink. "I'll check back next month when I come through. See if you're still here." He grabbed Harley's hand and shook it.

A faint sheen of moisture transferred from the trucker's sweaty palm to Harley's dry skin. The salt in Abe's perspiration seeped into Harley's raw bite marks and made them burn. Abe squeezed tight before he let go.

"Take care, son."

Rubbing his burning hand on his jeans to lessen the sting and the man's woodsy scent, Harley tried to devise a way to seduce Abe into giving up some blood. He knew he might not have such an easy opportunity again for days. He gave up when he realized he couldn't convince himself to make a move on the gruffly protective man.

Frustrated and angry at this new streak of unwanted

compassion, Harley threw himself against the door. He was out the truck without so much as a nod of thanks. He forced himself to not look back as he strode briskly away toward what appeared to be the heart of the little town.

Half a block later, he heard the truck rev up and slowly purr away. He shrugged his shoulders against the cold. The movement suddenly reminded him of the wood splinter in his back. It stung; the skin hot and irritated. Alone now, he felt emptier and more restless than he had in ages. The shadows seemed darker here, and the air more frigid. Maybe he was on the dark side of the moon.

The sounds of music and the smell of beer and sawdust reached him. A young couple emerged out of a building a few feet ahead of him, letting a blast of warmth grab Harley and tug him toward its source. He wanted to take advantage of his renewed desire for blood and he needed to find a willing bedmate to share the evening with. It was too late and he was too tired to find a room on his own tonight.

The sign in the front window proclaimed the bar to be the suggested "Sugar's". Harley captured the door as the couple slipped by him and wandered into the inviting depth of the small town bar, complete with beefy bartender, big screen TV and pool tables. It was nicely lit, not too dark, not too bright, and it smelled of oak, cue chalk and beer. Peanut shells littered the floor here and there and the jukebox played a slow country and western song Harley didn't recognize but liked. The singer's voice was low, deep and sensual, just the kind of voice he preferred.

He took a moment to let his eyes adjust to the room then wandered to the end of the bar and jostled between two guys to reach an empty stool. As he sat, he looked at the palm of the hand that Abe had shook, surprised by the burning sensation that still lingered on his skin. He sniffed his hand, perplexed by the strength of the earthy odor of the trucker.

Ordering a bottle of beer to keep up appearances, Harley slipped off the parka and then his leather jacket, letting them both fall over the low back of the barstool. Men on either side of him jostled his arms in an effort to grab their ordered drinks from the bartender, then drifted away to the pool tables and vinyl booths.

Tired, filled with a hunger that he couldn't name or quench, no matter how hard he tried to feed, Harley felt his whole body slump. His remaining energy drained away until he was boneless and empty. He wondered if he should just sit here and wait for his execution squad to find him. He just wished he didn't have to spend whatever was left of his life alone and feeling so...hollow. He knew he'd never have a chance at real love, but this was even worse— feeling nothing but emptiness.

He leaned against the stool's backrest, but the movement just intensified the burning between his shoulder blades. Instead of shifting forward and relieving the pressure on the wound, he pushed back and concentrated on the sharp stab of pain his action caused.

Eyes unfocused, staring blankly at some vague point across the room, mind lost in the numbing comfort of the wood-induced pain, Harley nearly fell off his seat when a silky voice rumbled near his ear.

"Yellow is a good color on you. Brings out the gold in your eyes."

The voice was so deep it vibrated all the way down to Harley's toes. The heat from the man's body actually reached out and touched Harley's chilled skin. The radical change in temperature, coupled with the man's heady scent, gave Harley gooseflesh.

"New in town, huh. Looks like you could use a friend."

The ailing vampire felt his ass clench and his cock stir from real desire for the first time in weeks. Before he turned his head to get a look at the stranger, he heard the man inhale deeply, sniffing Harley's hair and neck. Harley's cock hardened to a full erection and he fought the urge to reposition himself in his pants right there and then. He was surprised at the man's brazen actions in a public place, surrounded by neighborhood bar patrons, but delighted all the same. His fantasy lover from every wet dream he had ever entertained himself with over the decades danced through his mind. The image heightened his already stiff response.

Harley enjoyed the vision a moment longer then looked up, prepared to have his fantasy dashed to bits. No one could look as good as that voice sounded. His gaze met a brown flannel shirt spread over a well-formed chest that led to broad shoulders, a thick corded neck and one of the most attractive faces he had ever seen on a man.

The stranger was tall, brawny, and thirty-ish. His dark hair was neatly trimmed and his blue eyes were a pale shade that matched the turquoise thunderbird pendant that hung around his neck. The silver and stone piece lay against the tanned, supple flesh of the man's chest. The metal caught the light in brief flashes when the man breathed.

Harley lifted his gaze higher until it locked onto turquoise eyes. Like one of his own victims, caught in his vampire's thrall gaze, he felt unable to glance away.

The man was so close, Harley could hear the blood pulsing through his veins. His hunger rose and he licked his lips, automatically shoving his scarred hand into his mouth to stem the rapid rise of desire. He was just about to pierce his flesh when he realized there was no need to dampen his arousal.

Pretending to wipe away a phantom itch on his upper lip, Harley dropped his hand to his lap and shifted his hips forward. He'd practiced the move thousands of times and knew the pose defined the bulge of his erection against the threads of his tight jeans. He watched the man's gaze follow his lowering hand, pleased when the glance lingered at his crotch.

"Name's Matt. Matt Rush. I'm glad I decided to stay a little longer tonight. I was just on my way out the door."

Harley leaned closer to the man and covertly inhaled, drawing in the scent of male arousal mixed with an odd smell that he couldn't quite place. It was a little like Abe's but not so close that he would ever mistake them for each other. This scent turned him on and excited him, almost like a rush of fear did. Whatever it was, he craved it.

"You definitely give me a rush, I'll say that much for you, Matt." Harley looked up through the spiky fringe of his dark brown bangs with his best playful smile fixed on his lips. "My name's whatever you want it to be. And I can be very friendly."

He slowly thrust his pelvis forward another inch, spreading his thighs and forcing his jeans to pull more tightly across his lap. He could feel his cock jerk. Matt's sharp inhale of breath told him Matt had seen it.

"Just got into town. Looking for a place to stay." He rubbed his hand down his lap, letting his thumb run along the outline of his cock. "You know a place I can bed down for a night?" Matt's gaze followed every movement of Harley's hand, the stare so intense, Harley thought he could feel the heat from it on his groin. His desire stirred deeper, making him lightheaded with need and hunger.

"I might know a spot, maybe, yeah." The declaration from the big man was almost shy.

Warm puffs of air blew across Harley's cheek in rapid succession, making him realize that Matt was panting. The smell of arousal and need from the both of them was intoxicating. This was going to be quick and dirty, just the way Harley liked it. An attractive john and a warm place to sleep for the night. Things were looking up. Maybe his hunger would even last long enough for him to feed properly from this hunk of raw, walking sex appeal.

"I can pay." Harley slowly batted his long dark eyelashes at Matt. "Don't have much money, but," he flexed his thumb against the swollen head of his cock and felt the spot of wetness that had seeped through his pants. The movement drew Matt's gaze back down to Harley's groin.

A shiver of desire raced through Harley when he saw Matt's nostrils flare as if he had actually smelled the wet pre-cum the way the vampire could. "We could work out something, don't ya think?"

Matt snapped his gaze up from Harley's crotch, a soft, secretly amused smile on his lips. "Yeah, we could."

"Let's go then."

Like a light switch being flipped, Matt suddenly radiated an aura of confidence and authority. He took Harley by the arm and pulled the vampire off his seat, grabbing the falling coats and thrusting them to Harley's chest before the vampire's feet hit the ground.

"I've got a little place the next piece over. We can walk. Not much but it's quiet and it's mine." He eyed Harley from top to bottom and back again in a slow, sensual glance. "I know just the spot where you can stretch out." He turned toward the back exit and Harley hurried to follow, vaguely wondering who had just picked up whom.

§ § §

Unlike most bachelor places, Matt's house was clean and neat, furnished in genuine log cabin style with rough-textured wooden tables and sturdy, over-stuffed furniture. It smelt of apples and Matt's distinctive scent, one that Harley still couldn't place.

It was warm, cozy and made Harley wish he could leave. He didn't want to get comfortable here. Matt made him feel restless, aroused, and nervous, like a cornered animal. At the same time, he felt protected by the larger man's presence, something he'd never experienced before. It was amazing how being stalked and hunted like an animal by your own kind would make changes in the way you think.

As a vampire, he'd never needed protection or help from anyone else. At full strength, he could take on any john, even the ones twice his size. He could handle any problem. Any problem until a gun showed up as a new kind of sex toy.

There was a line of yellow symbols painted on the floor just past the entrance. Harley carefully stepped over them to grab hold of the back of a chair to steady himself as a wave of dizziness and nausea rippled through him. It was gone as fast as it hit. He leaned against the supporting piece of furniture and gestured at the floor paintings.

"The cafe where I got a ride had those same decorations on their floor. What's it mean? Some kind of Eskimo welcome?"

"There aren't any Eskimos here."

"You know what I mean, smartass."

"It's a kind of a local goodwill chant."

"Like a house blessing?"

"I guess you could call it that, yeah."

"Nice. Homey touch." If it weren't for the sarcasm, it would have been a nice compliment. Matt didn't seem to hear the intended insult or if he did, he didn't care.

"Thanks. I like it, but it gets lonely by myself." Matt closed and locked the door behind them.

The deadbolt sliding home made a sharp clicking sound and some of the fear and tension in Harley slipped away. A sense of being in a protected sanctuary struck the ailing vampire. He hated being so weak that he need help from an outside force to do what he couldn't do for himself anymore. It annoyed him and brought out his harsh, defensive side.

"I like being alone." His tone was hard and pointed. "Lot less trouble."

Matt merely winked at Harley, a knowing smile on his handsome, chiseled face. "I can handle a little trouble."

Matt's tone struck Harley as possessive, making Harley tense again. "I like my freedom. No chains for me. Ever."

"Uh huh." The irritating, secret smile stayed on Matt's face.

"Seriously." Harley moved further into the room to gain some distance from his soon-to-be bedmate of the moment. "What's it get you?"

"Well, let's see." Matt tossed his keys onto the fireplace mantle then turned back to stare into Harley's eyes. "Companionship, acceptance, protection. Maybe even love?"

Taken back by the intensity of Matt's gaze, Harley swallowed down the bitter reply he'd had on his tongue and muttered, "Right." It was a struggle but, after a moment, he managed to break away from the mesmerizing teal-colored stare.

Moving to the center of the living area, Harley stood in the middle of a braided circular rug and looked up. A small square skylight showed the starlit sky. A portion of the ever-present moon showed its full face and cratered complexion. Harley slowly spun in a small circle as he examined the ring of symbols painted around the skylight with a perplexed stare. Though they were the same type of symbols as on the floor, these were blue and seemed different somehow.

"You even put a blessing on your ceiling?" He threw Matt a twisted grin. "You're even weirder than I am." He looked at the skylight again, then glanced around the room, noticing the lack of any furniture under or near it. "Wouldn't it be more useful over the bed? Where you could actually watch the sky?"

"Trust me, it's perfect right where it's at."

After a pause Harley shrugged and mumbled. "Just as well. Didn't fancy watching the sun come up anyway. Even if there was one around here right now."

Slipping off both coats, Harley threw them onto the nearest chair, smirking when Matt immediately scooped them up off the furniture and hung them on the hooks by the door.

Matt hung his own jacket beside Harley's. He paused and ran a hand slowly down the sleeve of the yellow parka, his nose only inches from the fabric. After a deep breath he released the coat sleeve and slipped out of his boots, leaving them neatly on a small mat by the door.

Once again Harley got a chance to admire the man's solid, well-muscled body in better lighting. From the top of his brown-haired head to the tip of his socked feet the man was gorgeous, obviously athletic and powerfully built. Fantasy man come to life.

Resisting a sigh, Harley promised himself he'd leave unannounced in a day or two. In the meantime, he'd enjoy the moment, like always. He couldn't hope for more than an isolated moment of affection and comfort. A vampire could never have more than that. He tore his gaze away from Matt's body and looked at his new surroundings. He slipped off his wet boots, leaving them in the middle of the room.

The house had an open floor plan that let Harley see into every corner. The fireplace in the living area still had embers glowing in the hearth. Past a small eat-in kitchen, the back half of the room had been transformed into a bedroom.

A king-sized bed dominated the far corner, box springs and mattress supported on a thick wooden platform that prevented things from getting shoved underneath it. It was covered in a thick pile of blankets with a down comforter folded up against the slatted footboard. It looked soft, warm and inviting. Harley hoped the sheets were clean. For some reason, he didn't want to smell any other lovers but Matt in his bed tonight.

The rising scent of hormones in the air from both of them told Harley they were wasting time on pleasantries.

"Guess it's time to pay the rent, huh?"

Without another word he stripped the thin Henley shirt off his torso and tossed it on the floor. His hands went immediately to his belt and snap but two larger hands clamped over his from behind, stilling them before he could get his zipper down.

"Let me do it."

It was a deep, breathy command that made the hair on Harley's neck rise. "Sure, if that's what gets you off, gorgeous."

Harley shivered at Matt's touch as the large hands moved up to rest on his shoulders. The touch was gentle but firm, holding Harley in place, but he still flinched when Matt's fingers found the inflamed skin around the embedded wood between his shoulder blades.

"You've got a cut here."

"Just a piece of wood. Couldn't reach it. It'll work its way out eventual— Shit!" A sharp pain stabbed through his back and Harley jerked forward, but Matt's hand on his shoulder held him in place.

"It's out." A gentle touch soothed over the inflamed skin. "Looks infected though."

"I don't get infections." Flexing his shoulders, Harley could tell the wood was gone. The ache and burn were gone too, leaving only a dull throb and a small area of heat. It was still more discomfort than he should have been able to feel. Sighing he admitted, "At least not until recently. It'll be okay."

"This will help."

A wet lap of tongue over the spot made Harley jump but he didn't pull away. It felt good. "You sure you want to do that?"

Matt didn't answer, just continued to lick at the wound, even nibbling at the edges. When he was done, he pulled Harley firmly back to rest against him.

Feeling the heat of arousal rise as Matt pressed against the length of his back, Harley closed his eyes and enjoyed the warmth. He felt good for the first time in days. Even the wound on his back no longer burned. Matt began to massage his shoulders, working out the stiff muscles of Harley's neck and upper back.

The vampire relaxed under the heavy touch, fighting an odd impulse to escape the intimacy. He'd never shied away from a partner before. The urge to run hit him hard, then melted away when wet, nuzzled kisses brushed over his neck and up into his dark hair. He bit off a sigh and leaned back, letting Matt take the majority of his weight. Suddenly the self-imposed isolation of his entire existence paled and an unrecognizable ache bloomed under his breast. He tensed again.

Matt pressed his body more firmly against Harley, his warm breath bathing Harley's neck and sending shivers across his skin.

The tension in his body eased once more. Harley allowed his head to fall back onto a broad shoulder. Matt brought his cheek to rest against Harley's, the rough texture of a day's growth of beard prickling against Harley's sensitive skin. The burn sent a flash of desire straight to the vampire's already hard cock. Harley kept his eyes closed and panted to keep his arousal under control.

He inhaled deeply and drew in the scent of the man, earthy and primal, and something else he couldn't quite remember yet. The alien sensation of being cared for and sheltered accompanied the smell. Rather than making him bolt for a door and freedom, this time a shudder of need rolled through his body so powerful it made him gasp.

Matt slid his hands off of Harley's shoulders and down his back to his hips. Rubbing gently at the sensitive skin just above the waistline of Harley's jeans, Matt gradually worked his fingers along the fabric until the snap of Harley's fly was in his hands. Matt eased the snap open and lowered the zipper, sliding the loose fabric slowly down. There were no briefs under the jeans.

"Let me help." Harley shimmied his hips, but strong arms grabbed them, stopping the seductive dance.

"I've got it. Let me." It was a throaty command, almost a growl, full of restrained need and want.

A shudder of desire raced down Harley's spine, but he made his voice flip and playful. "Okay by me. If you want to."

"I want to." Matt intensified his caress, trailing a line of kisses down Harley's spine and across each buttock as the globes of pale flesh were revealed. Strong hands roved over every inch of his chest and abdomen, then slid down his legs to push the abandoned jeans the rest of the way off.

Matt slowly dropped to the floor with the pants. While the fabric pooled around Harley's ankles, Matt caressed and stroked over Harley's sides and outside of his thighs. He buried his face in the small of Harley's back and puffed hot breaths into the dip of his spine, sending shivers of anticipation through the vampire.

Wrapping his left arm around Harley's waist, Matt massaged his way down Harley's right leg, deftly easing jeans and socks off. He repeated the slow, sensual process with the left leg, then stroked his way back up to rest his hands on Harley's abdomen.

Matt effortlessly rose from his knees, keeping a hand on Harley's belly, fingers combing through the fine, dark hairs growing there. Matt's other hand swirled up Harley's back, callused fingertips moving over the smooth skin of his shoulder blades. The hand ran down Harley's spine a dozen leisurely times before Matt suddenly stepped away to quickly shrug out of his own layers of clothing.

Nude, Matt slipped his arms around Harley's chest from behind again and pulled him backward to press tightly against his body. Settling his growing erection firmly against Harley's cheeks, he returned his attention to Harley's neck, nibbling and nipping the sensitive flesh until Harley squirmed and hissed.

The room spun. Harley found himself clamped chest to chest with Matt, a fire of raw need and lust burning in the man's heated gaze. It matched his own raging desires. He pulled Matt's head down, pressing his lips hard to the welcoming mouth.

He twisted in Matt's arms, trying to gain a better hold on the tall, virile man. Lacing the fingers of both hands through the man's thick hair, Harley sealed their mouths more firmly together, a groan of real desire escaping him.

So engrossed in the delicious sensations of Matt's dominant tongue exploring every contour of his mouth, Harley barely noticed when he was lifted off the floor. He realized he was weightless for a millisecond before he landed in the middle of the bed and Matt's weight settled over him, pinning him in place. He wasn't sure how they got there, but it never interrupted their kiss.

Returning each of Matt's caresses stroke for stroke, Harley explored the hard-muscled body pressing him into the mattress. He was thrilled by the barely restrained energy the big man radiated in every electric touch.

Harley broke away from the kiss to study Matt's face. Passion and longing burned in the depths of Matt's hypnotic eyes and scorched a blazing path of desire straight through to Harley's cock. Harley darted up to recapture Matt's mouth in a demanding kiss, eager to take back a little control in their coupling, but Matt overwhelmed him again and Harley surrendered.

It was an old game. Harley didn't like the Dom/sub scene but he knew how to play it. And in this case, the role might be worth it, even if it was real life.

After long moments of breathless exploration and teasing, Matt broke away to lavish feather-light kisses across Harley's closed eyelids and flushed face. His gentle ministrations were quickly rewarded with small gasps of pleasure and the thrusting of Harley's hips. Matt added tiny, sharp nibbles and soothing laps of his tongue to the assault on Harley's senses.

"Christ, Matt." Harley's thrusts became more rhythmic. He ground his full erection against Matt's answering arousal, hands skimming restlessly over the larger man's arms and chest. "Come on, man. Do it."

"Not yet."

"Why?" Under other circumstances, Harley would have been embarrassed by the whine in his voice.

"Not until I know your name." Matt took Harley's face between his hands and stared into his eyes. "Your real name." The burning gaze intensified. "I'll know if you're lying." His voice was deep and guttural, almost playful, but his eyes held a distinctly serious gleam.

Staring into the teal eyes, a minuscule tremble shook through Harley's smaller, pinned frame and he found his own response came out unsure. "No you won't."

Without dropping his gaze from Harley's, Matt merely dipped his head slightly as if he was taking a firmer stand. "Try me."

Harley stared into Matt's face, studying his features, trying to decide what it was he found so compelling about the rugged man. It wasn't just his good looks. There was something primal and wild about him that both excited Harley and made him nervous. And defensive. "What difference does it make?"

Placing a chaste kiss on Harley's out-thrust chin, Matt stroked over Harley's jawline with his thumbs while still holding the vampire's face immobile. "I want to know your name before we join."

"Join?" Harley snorted and tried to turn his head away. This was nothing more than a no-strings-attached bump and grind. The way Matt said 'join' gave the act a lot more meaning than it really had. He didn't know why, but it made him uncomfortable. "It's only sex." He squirmed but couldn't move under Matt's weight.

"It's only a name."

Again the deep voice sent a thrill through him that rocketed to his groin and made his cock ache with neglect. Something about Matt made Harley respond to him on an instinctive level. Unable to pinpoint it, he finally just gave up searching for an answer. His blood lust was rising along with his frustrated libido. He wasn't willing to spend any more time on the mystery. "Christ, okay. Harley. My name's Harley."

"Harley." A smile split across Matt's face and Harley was stunned by the way it transformed the handsome face into a gorgeous one. The man's dark hair was mussed, and strands fell forward framing his tanned face. It made his eyes seem larger and almost luminescent. "Rhymes with snarly. Fits you."

Peeved at himself for giving in, but not really expecting an answer, Harley demanded, "Need the last name too?"

"I know that one." Matt gave a small shake of his head.

"No, you don't."

Matt's hips begun making tiny circles that pressed his firm, heavy cock into Harley's trapped shaft, distracting him. He grunted in frustration when his own hips rose up to increase the contact, seemingly on their own.

"What is it then?"

"Doesn't matter what it is now. When we're done here tonight, it'll be 'Rush'."

"You're delusional." Harley snorted again, but the calm, decisive look in Matt's eyes made him shiver and pause for a moment. He tried to laugh it off as all part of the bizarre seduction game that came with bedding complete strangers. Some just turned out to be crazier than others.

"Whatever makes the fantasy work for you, guy." But his voice trembled and an odd, fluttery feeling settled in his stomach. He pretended it was just his need to feed.

"Wait and see, Harley."

Without another word, Matt renewed his attack on Harley's body, suckling, nipping, lapping and rubbing at every sensitive area Harley knew existed on the human body. He gradually worked his way to Harley's straining erection. He lapped at the crease between Harley's groin and one thigh, delicately running a rough tongue over the sensitive crease. Wrapping his arms around Harley's slender hips, Matt pulled him closer and kneaded the taut muscles of Harley's ass.

Pushing conversation from his thoughts, Harley moaned and his hands wandered restlessly through Matt's hair, stroking his face and rubbing at his scalp. He thrust up and then pulled away, confused by his own needs. He wasn't like this with johns. He didn't respond to every touch and caress like it was the first one he had ever had, but tonight he didn't need any of his patented fake moans or groans. Matt brought out his true sex drive and kicked it into high gear.

He buried his hands in the mass of thick hair on Matt's head, following the path of Matt's head as it dipped and swayed, licking over every square inch of Harley's taut stomach and groin. Just when he was sure Matt was going to give him the best blowjob of his life, the phone on the bedside table rang.

On the second ring, an answering machine in the living area picked up. A woman's voice drifted to them, but neither stopped what they were doing.

"Deputy Rush? I know you like the night shift best, even on your days off, so I didn't think it would hurt to call now. Thought maybe I could catch you at home." A sigh of disappointment reached across the line. "Anyway, Chief Miller wanted me to call and remind you that you agreed to take Deputy Logan's shift tomorrow night so he can attend the Sheriff's Ball. Sorry you're not going. I was hoping to see you there." Another longing sigh. "Bye, Deputy."

Harley ignored the first few words from the disembodied voice, concentrating on the delicious feeling of Matt's tongue on his balls instead. Ignored them right up until their meaning crashed through his sex-addled brain.

"FUCK!" Harley rocketed up and scrambled to pull his lower half out from under Matt's restraining weight. The strong hands clamped around his hips dug in deep and held on tight while Matt dragged Harley bodily back down.

"Jesus, motherfucking, son of a bitching COP!" Harley kicked and snarled, squirming with all of his remaining vampire strength, livid and outraged with betrayal. "You goddamned, fucking bastard!"

"Just wait a damn minute, Harley!"

Ignoring the firm command, he swung a punch at Matt's head and was rewarded by having both his wrists pinned to the mattress, each one encased in a firm grip and planted squarely down by his shoulders where he couldn't get any leverage to twist away. If there had been a scant chance that feeding from the man would have increased his chances of escape, Harley would have bitten Matt.

As it was, he couldn't even get his head up off the mattress. His vampire strength wasn't completely gone, but even with it he was overpowered and helpless in Matt's grip, pinned under the hard-muscled, sculptured body and pressed into the soft, clean bed. Harley supposed there were worse ways to get arrested for solicitation. But this one was going to be a bitch to talk his way out of.

He had actually forgotten about all the reasons he had picked up Matt in the first place.

"Just stop fighting me and listen, damn it."

Despite his anger, Matt's voice sent a tingle of anticipation through Harley's still eager body. He stopped struggling and lay panting, staring defiantly up at his captor.

He couldn't read the look on Matt's face, but the scent of increasing arousal was heady in the air. It seemed a little struggle turned them both on. Handcuffs might be in his immediate future, but he didn't think arresting him was on the man's mind.

"Fuck!"

"We were about to." Matt dipped his head down and claimed Harley's tense lips until they parted for him. "Even cops have sex, enjoy sex, Harley."

He kissed Harley's eyelids closed. "And I'm off duty." Then his nose and each cheek, the touch a light brush that made Harley's skin gooseflesh.

"On my own time. With you." He nipped at Harley's chin, then soothed it with a lick. "Right where I'm supposed to be. Where I want to be."

Cutting off any comment Harley might make, Matt captured the vampire's mouth. He thoroughly explored it with his tongue and lips until Harley knew Matt could tell how many teeth the vampire had.

The urge to drop his fangs made his jaw ache, but he held back. Matt had already proven he was more than a match for Harley in the fight department. He knew he was weakened, but not so far gone that a man, even a brawny, muscular man, should be able to overpower him. His end was definitely near. So why ruin what was proving to be a great night of sex? Harley moaned and relaxed, surrendering.

The hold on his wrists didn't lessen at first, but Matt leaned in and attacked every erogenous zone Harley owned. First he bit the soft skin of Harley's neck hard enough the vampire knew it would leave a mark. It sent a flush of pleasure to blaze along his nerve endings. A trail of enticing caresses and soft, wet, nibbling kisses mapped out the contours of his torso and groin.

Just as Harley felt himself ready to explode, a strong touch encircled the root of his cock and a firm pressure dampened the fire to a dull ache.

"Not so fast, Harley." While keeping a firm grip in place to quell Harley's pending climax, Matt kissed the tip of Harley's shaft, lapping at the underside of the reddened cap, tasting the sampling of pre-cum collecting in the slit. Harley would have suggested a condom, but he knew the man couldn't catch anything from him. Vampires didn't carry infections. Usually.

Licking his way around the spongy head, Matt bathed the sensitive tip in saliva then suckled it dry again. Turning his grip into a slow massage up and down the hard shaft, he began to stroke over the sac beneath it. Harley's hips moved in time to the rhythm.

Smoothing the traces of saliva and pre-cum over Harley's cock, Matt aligned their bodies. He lowered himself to rest his weight fully on Harley until their arousals slid against each other. The slightest motion sent waves of sizzling lust up Harley's spine.

Harley moaned, then bit his lip when it brought a smile to Matt's lips. Ducking down to capture the sound with his mouth, Matt delivered a deep kiss that stole both the moan and Harley's breath away.

Propping himself up on his elbows on either side of Harley's chest, Matt began to grind and thrust into Harley in a breath-taking dance of pure lustful need. Harley responded to the explosive rhythm and matched it.

Matt gracefully shifted off Harley's body to settle between his legs. He captured Harley's pleasure-glazed stare in his own and then swallowed Harley's erection to the base. Matt sucked and swallowed, using one hand to hold Harley's writhing hips to the mattress and the other to caress the soft skin around his spread ass. Harley grunted and rocked as Matt ran a finger over the skin between Harley's scrotum and the opening to his body.

Nearing the edge of climax, Harley moaned and bucked as Matt worked a spit-covered finger roughly into Harley's opening. Matt released Harley's shaft and began to lick and nip at it as he worked two more fingers in. Matt angled every hard thrust of his hand to rub over Harley's prostate, making him shudder with pain-tinged pleasure. One hand massaged Harley's tight sac as he worked his fingers in and out, establishing a rhythm of stroking and thrusts.

"Come on fantasy man, do me!" Harley literally vibrated with tension, his body screaming with the need. He needed to come, he needed to feed and he needed for this not to end.

Suddenly his orientation shifted as his position changed. Before he knew it he was kneeling on the bed on all fours, ass in the air, hips held in place by Matt's powerful hands. His knees were shoved apart and a slicked, iron-hard poker of heated flesh jabbed at the waiting entrance to his body. His asshole puckered and clenched at the intrusion, then grasped the thick shaft as it inched in and pulled out in a smooth, slippery slide of hard flesh on flesh.

"Fuck!"

Once again his body was suddenly lifted and repositioned. Pulled back onto Matt's thickly muscled thighs, Harley found himself in Matt's lap, ass filled with every inch of the other man's cock. Strong arms embraced him from behind, clasping his back tightly to Matt's broad chest.

A hand brushed over his nipples, tweaking and rubbing them to stiff peaks. They burned and crinkled, erect and excited. His cock jutted out from between his widespread thighs, knees bent and calves held apart by Matt's. The moderate growth of dark coarse hair on the man's legs and groin brushed against sensitive areas of Harley's ass and inner thighs and the sweet, teasing friction made his cock ache with need.

The sliding pressure in his ass sent jolts of electric pleasure up his spine with each thrust. An added little twist of Matt's hip at the end of the thrust hit Harley's prostate every now and then. Each hit made his vision blur and the room dim. If it had been on target with each thrust, Harley was sure he'd have passed out from it. The stretch and burn at his opening each time Matt plunged deep enough that his cock was buried to its stout, flared base sent a special thrill straight to Harley's brain.

His hair was grabbed and his head was gently but forcibly bent back. Matt's earthy scent filled Harley's nose and mouth. He could almost taste the rich tang of the man's blood. The smell was pungent, full of sweat and hormones with a touch of something Harley still could not identify. The smell piqued his arousal like nothing else ever had.

Matt nipped and licked the length of Harley's exposed neck, raising blood to the surface with a few overly sharp bites.

The rough play pushed Harley's blood lust higher and he reached for his cock to sate at least one of his body's needs. Before they could reach their goal, both his hands were snapped up and captured in Matt's square palms.

"I got this one, lover. It's all on me."

Matt spread his thighs, forcing Harley's to open wider as well. He clasped Harley's wrists in one hand and held the vampire's arms to his chest in an unyielding embrace. Cock barely leaving Harley's body, Matt began a series of rapid thrusts, each movement pressing his shaft deeper and deeper, stretching the nerve-filled ring of guardian muscle and sliding unerringly over the swollen nub of Harley's prostate.

"Satan's son! Bastard!" Harley writhed and bucked.

The stimulation sent spasms through him, shivers and bolts of feelings so intense Harley could only describe them as surreal. He grunted and moaned, his cock iron-hard, a deep hue of red that told him where most of his scant blood supply was currently circulating. His nipples burned, the bites on his neck scalded his skin, his wrists hurt, his mind reeled and his ass had become the focus of his entire world. He felt full, electric, terrified, restless and exhausted, and he needed something to bite. He needed to touch his cock, to get that last bit of pressure, stimulation, contact, to push him over the edge, but Matt wouldn't let go of him. In this position, he wasn't close enough to anything to bite.

"Bastard, bastard, bastard!"

He was going to burst into flame any minute now, he was sure of it. He bucked and squirmed trying to free himself from Matt's hold, needing release but not really wanting to leave Matt's arms. He didn't want this to end, but it had to. He needed to come and he needed to feed. He'd lose his mind if he didn't.

Throwing his head back, Harley tossed it from side to side, trying unsuccessfully to make some kind of contact with Matt's body. A ridge of flesh, a fold of skin, anything he could sink his fangs into for a taste. All he could handle anymore was a small taste, and he needed it more now than he had in all his decades as a vampire.

Suddenly, hot lips pressed to the bullet scar on his temple and the room swam as a wave of dizziness crashed over him. A sharp cry of pain escaped him, then a beefy wrist was jammed into his open mouth before he could pull his head away.

Harley didn't even think about what he was doing before his fangs descended and he was slurping and gulping down mouthful after mouthful of rich, slick blood. His swallows were in time to the deep thrusts in his ass. He came as the first droplets of blood coated his tongue, a pulsing thin stream of pink-tinged cum that splashed his flat, pale abdomen and lean thighs, filling the air with the scent of his own release, nearly overwhelming the taste of the ambrosia on his lips and in his mouth.

Matt's human heartbeat pounded through the man's broad, sweaty chest and thumped against Harley's back in time to his swallows. A flood of heated cum suddenly shot up his ass, the fluid burning every cell it touched, creating a chain reaction of building pleasure as more and more of it spread into his body, absorbed and channeled to his nervous system, enveloping his every fiber in an erotic seizure of pleasure and passion. Even the insistent, wet tongue strokes against his head wound became tolerable. He had no idea what just happened to him, but it left him euphoric and dazed.

His stomach growled with pleasure. Harley couldn't stop himself from drinking more. He didn't take time to question why the wrist had been offered or why it continued to be offered without a struggle. They all struggled at the first bite, but he could keep his victims cooperative with a hypnotic gaze and distracting lick of their cock, or a shift and jut of his talented ass. He could do none of those things right now, and yet the wrist remained at his lips.

He used both hands to grasp the sinewy arms holding him tightly to Matt's muscular body, desperate for the moment to continue no matter what the reason. Despite the pain he knew his teeth were causing, Matt kept his wrist pressed firmly to Harley's lips.

Swallowing down a final gulp of the rich, exotic tasting blood, Harley barely registered Matt's second release inside of him. Unusually groggy with the newly gorged-on blood, he regretted when Matt's still hard cock slid from his ass, leaving him awash with a hollow, lonely feeling. His eyes fluttered closed and when he forced them back open, he was lying on his back on the bed, his head propped up on a soft pillow, legs splayed out on either side of Matt's kneeling body as it loomed over him. His wrists were again encased in Matt's grip, one on either side of his hips.

Harley licked the last of the blood from his lips, savoring the familiar yet unidentifiable and unique flavor of the man. Eyelids heavy with a strange euphoric feeling that battled with his predatory vampiric nature, Harley shivered and twitched. Fear, excitement, pleasure—he wasn't sure what it was, but it buffeted his senses and confused him.

Fangs still absentmindedly descended, he smiled up at a waiting Matt and licked his lips again, Matt's flavor becoming more distinct and recognizable.

"You taste good."

His eyelids drooped and he forced them wide again to stare up at Matt's face. The man looked smug and slightly expectant, as if he was waiting for Harley to say something more. The vampire obliged, a sleepy, indistinct mutter to his words.

"You taste…I don't know, kind of—wild. Primal." He raked his teeth over his tongue, reawakening the lingering tang of rich blood. "Kinda scares me a little, but it makes me feel good, too." He closed his eyelids and searched his brain for a name to describe the taste. It was on the tip of his tongue, he just needed to concentrate. "Powerful and woodsy. Reminds me of a wild beast in the forest."

Eyelids popping open, Harley blinked at the

shimmering vision of Matt's looming, naked body in front of him. Matt's dark hair was mussed, his broad shoulders flexed as he knelt between Harley legs, bent forward slightly to pin Harley's wrists to the bed down low on the mattress, cock still long and thick and hard, proudly jutting up between them.

Matt was masterful, gorgeous and delicious. Even now the scent of the man's blood filled the air and teased Harley's darker desires. Harley's long dead soul stirred in his chest and he swore his still heart gave a thunderous beat. He frowned, giving an unwilling voice to his thoughts.

"You're—" About to reveal the sudden rush of uncharacteristic emotion and longing for the man, Harley faltered as a name for Matt's flavor finally popped into this head. "You're...lycan!"

"Jesus, holy fuck, son of Satan, son a bitcccch!" Harley jerked and kicked, flinging his head and bucking, scrambling and convulsing to escape Matt's relentless, unyielding grip. "Christ almighty, motherfucker, spawn of the devil's dog, let me go!" He spat on the floor, trying to rid his mouth of the taste of his lover, more for spite than from a desire to have it gone.

"Bastard, bastard, bastard! Werewolf! Heathen bastard!" He twisted, jerked, writhed and arched but he never gained an inch of freedom.

Matt waited until Harley had nearly exhausted himself then slowly lowered his body until they were chest to chest and face to face.

"And you're vampire."

"No shit!" Defiant, Harley licked a smear of blood from his lips, then grinned around his still extended fangs. "What was your first clue, Deputy?"

Pulling one of Harley's bitten and scarred hands off the bed, Matt examined it more closely. A frown marred his handsome face as he ran a thumb over the tortured skin. "A sick vampire."

He tucked the hand down under the combined weight of both their bodies, then used his free hand to brush Harley's sweaty bangs aside to reveal the healing bullet wound. "You survived a bullet wound to the head without bleeding out. Tough one, even for a vampire. That's one for the books, isn't it?"

All his concern and caring was met with a fierce glare and silence from Harley, until Matt touched the wound and Harley gasped and jerked his head away.

"Still hurts?" Matt's frown deepened. His fingers brushed over the wound again.

This time it didn't hurt quite as much but Harley still buried the side of his face in the pillow to minimize the contact. He'd have bitten Matt's fingers if he didn't think his already too-full stomach would rebel at receiving more blood.

Retreating from Harley's wound, Matt used his hand to turn the vampire's face back to him. "Mangled your senses didn't it? You really didn't know I was lycan until you tasted my blood. I would never have believed it if I hadn't seen it for myself. You are something special,

Harley."

Harley blinked at the look of awe in Matt's eyes and in his voice. No one else so far had thought his surviving had been anything but a freak living through a freak attack. The admiration was disconcerting. The look of affection and pride in Matt's eyes was highly disturbing. That flopping sensation inside his chest happened again and he swore he felt a beat under his rib cage. The whole moment made him speechless.

When Harley didn't respond, Matt added, "I can make it better."

"What?"

"The pain from the bullet wound." He jutted his chin at the scar. "I can make it better faster, over time. Just like the wound on your back."

Harley flexed his shoulders and realized the burn from the splinter was completely gone as if it had never been there. He gave Matt a narrowed eye glare. "How'd you do that?"

"In each pack there is one who is the healer. I've been given the gift in mine."

Searching the room as if more werewolves were going to spring from the closets, Harley demanded, "Where's the rest of them?"

"Not close. I've been on my own here for a year or so. Waiting for my mate to arrive." He stroked tenderly over Harley's lips, playfully rubbing the tips of his fangs in the process. "And now you have."

He kissed the tip of Harley's chin and nuzzled his neck while his hips began to slide over Harley's, hard cock. The action smeared the fluid from their combined releases into each other's skin.

Speech edged with a harsh sarcasm and the hesitant confusion caused by exhaustion, Harley relaxed nonetheless, allowing himself to enjoy the little kisses and soft caresses Matt lavished on his sensitive neck. "I'm on the run, crazy man. Away from people, not to them. And especially not to a furball like you. Animal."

Matt ignored the half-hearted insult and probed for more information. "From the guy that did this?"

"No." It came out as more of a snort than a word. "He's long dead." Harley tried to look at Matt, to gauge what the man/werewolf was thinking, but his eyelids wouldn't cooperate. He hadn't felt this tired in decades, if ever. "I've got bigger problems than that asshole."

"Vampire hunters?"

His whole world had narrowed down to Matt's strong, inquisitive voice and Harley responded to it without wanting to. He wanted to sleep instead. God, he hated feeling this weak.

"Worse. Vampire vampire hunters." He sighed and licked his lips, absently noting that his fangs had receded along with his ability to stay awake. "Eliminators."

"Whoa!"

The surprise was there, but Harley had expected it to be more pronounced and panicked. The thought of the assassins panicked him. Usually. Just not right now for some reason.

"Yeah. So get off me. I gotta go." Not a single muscle in his body responded besides his tongue. That didn't get him off the bed or out from under Matt's reassuring weight.

"You need me."

"You can't help, he-man." Harley yawned and his eyes fluttered. He forced them open suddenly, but they dropped closed again as Matt's soothing warmth continued to soak into him. "I need a miracle, not a werewolf." It was a slurred, mumbled protest.

"How much time have we got?"

"One night, maybe two." Harley stirred and pushed feebly at Matt's hands, eyelids still closed. "Now let me go. Gotta leave soon." His head dropped low then, wobbly, bobbed back up with an indignant outburst. "And we don't have any time. I travel alone remember?"

"Not any more, Harley. Unlike vampires, wolves protect their own."

The whispered words tickled his ear and sent a shiver down his spine, promise and threat rolled into one.

"I'm not yours." Harley fought a yawn and lost.

"So you keep saying."

A light kiss landed on his lips, then Matt's tongue parted Harley's lips and teased over his sensitive fangs almost making them drop again. Harley suppressed a moan and clamped his mouth shut. He'd have bitten the irritating werewolf if he didn't know the taste of lycan's blood would raise his libido again. His cock would willingly stay up, but he couldn't.

"Fuck you."

The snort of laughter tickled just as much as the breathy whisper had.

"We'll see. Maybe."

Soothing one last lick and kiss over the healing bullet wound scar, Matt moved up to peck little kisses over Harley's pale face. He petted the disarrayed, shaggy hair back from Harley's forehead and stroked a hand through the strands, tenderly ghosting his fingers over the bullet wound.

For once, Harley didn't even jerk away or protest. He'd never admit it out loud, but it felt kind of good.

Shifting his weight to one side, Matt pulled an unresisting and heavy- limbed Harley on top of him and settled the smaller body into the crook of his side. Harley automatically held on.

Arms entwined, Matt snagged a blanket and pulled it up to cover Harley's chilled body. Running a hand through Harley's hair, Matt nudged Harley's head until it was nestled comfortably on his chest and waited.

"Fucking furball." Exasperated, Harley patted down the section of Matt's thick, dark chest hair to keep it from tickling his nose, then drew another breath to protest the entire move, but faded off to sleep before it escaped his lips.

§ § §

His dreams were about midnight runs and moonlight seductions, full of sex and complex emotions he'd rather not explore. The amazing part wasn't so much the feelings the dreams evoked in Harley as it was the fact that he was having them at all. His last dream had been when he was twenty-three and still human, thirty years ago. Back then he had wanted mundane things like a nice apartment, an ordinary job and a lover to share it all with who wouldn't care he had been a hustler before meeting him. All those dreams died when he had, and life as a vampire hadn't afforded him any new ones.

Although these dreams didn't include ordinary events like his old ones, the feelings of contentment, of being needed and loved, were much the same. Though he couldn't visualize anyone else in the dream with him, every one of his senses told him the underlying reason for the happiness was the man he'd just had sex with— made love with, if he was being honest. Matt's scent and presence was the one prevailing factor throughout the dreams. The realization irritated him to no end and thrilled him unlike anything had in decades.

Contentment was a loser's game he couldn't afford to let himself be lulled into. Subconsciously aware of the danger of attachments in his troubled, waning existence, Harley fought happiness at every turn, even in this rediscovered dream. The ground he was peacefully lying on shook and the cloak of comfort and dream-fueled bliss shattered around him. Harsh reality invaded his death sleep and yanked him awake prematurely.

Still groggy from both his sexual and physical appetites being sated for the first time in way too long, Harley jerked awake to a thunderous growl of a wild animal. Jackknifing to an upright position, he found himself alone, naked, tangled in the sheets of Matt's bed.

By the footboard stood a dark haired, massive, muscle-bound werewolf. It growled deep in its throat, the sound so raw, powerful and vicious it made the hair on Harley's arms and neck stand on end. He knew instinctively this was Matt in his other form, but all the same, he was relieved to see the lycan's attention was riveted on the overhead skylight and not him.

"Matt?"

Nothing but a low growl answered him, but Harley knew it was meant as a warning to be silent. Managing to untangle himself enough to rise to his knees, he watched as Matt swiftly stooped and whisked the round braided rug from the floor, to reveal a blue circle of symbols that matched the ones around the skylight directly about them. The rug flew across the room to land in a heap under a window. As it smacked the wall and slid to the floor, Harley noticed symbols painted on the windowsill, yellow like the ones by the front door.

He tried to untangle his legs from the sheets, but failed before the skylight burst inward, blanketing the room with a thousand shards of tinted glass. The room seemed to explode with noise, shattered wood and rumbled growls as two indistinct, but familiar dark-clothed bodies hurtled down through the narrow opening, one after the other.

In battle stance, crossbows in hand and ready, the two snarling Eliminators landed gracefully on their feet. Ignoring everything else, it took them less than a millisecond to zero in on Harley where he knelt, trapped in the sheets, on the end of Matt's bed. Both fired their weapons at the same time. Oblivious, Harley tried to blink away the sleep and watch the action in the room.

Shifted into full lycan form, Matt was a fearsome sight. Easily a foot taller than when in his human shape, he became broader, thicker and decidedly more intimidating in looks alone. Add in the vicious, rumbling growl that shook the house rafters, to the wicked slash of his extended, massive claws and five-inch canines, he put the Eliminators' merely over-sized human fangs and ordinary builds to shame. Even their vampire strength and lightning reflexes couldn't save them.

As the vampires took aim, Matt lunged forward, knocking one crossbow down with his foot while he tore the other from the nearest vampire's grip with his hands. He took the vampire's arm as well, amputating it from the tall, angular one's shoulder with the force of the impact. He used the momentary surprise to tear out the vamp's throat, then snapped his spine at the neck, severing the head from body. In one smooth move, he threw the head onto the discarded rug under the window, then hefted the body and tossed it after its owner. It only took a second for the body parts to disintegrate into ash and scatter on the floor like so much dust.

Harley watched in amazement, the whole scene

occurring faster than his sleep-addled brain could comprehend it. A sudden burning in his side drew his bleary gaze downward and he noticed for the first time there was an arrow lodged under his left rib cage. The shaft was made of white ash and it literally burned his flesh.

Hissing as a tendril of smoke rose from the fresh wound, Harley managed to snap one end off the arrow. A swift yank and he'd tugged the shaft out of his side, surprised at how little it actually hurt. He was shocked when it began to heal, slower than it should have for a vampire, but much faster than he had been healing.

He jerked wider awake, his gaze jumping back to the center of the room where Matt stood looming over the remaining vampire. This was the one that had stood at the cafe door and waited for Harley to come to him. Obviously of a more patient disposition than his partner had been, he again stood and just waited, empty crossbow pointed at the floor.

"You're healing again." More observant and calmer than expected with an enraged lycan sniffing his throat, the remaining vampire nodded at Harley's side. "How?" His narrowed gaze swung between Matt and Harley, than landed on Matt. "You? You did this?"

"Lycan protect their own."

"He's Vampyre not Lycan!" The Eliminator spit on the floor and snarled, "We take care of our own."

Matt bared his teeth. "We don't destroy our injured." He stepped closer to the edge of the circle and growled, deep in his throat. The glass in one window rattled. "We care for them until they are strong again, as he will be soon enough. Remember that, assassin."

"He's still not a Lycan." It came out between gritted teeth, fangs extended and glistening in the moonlight shining in from the hole in the ceiling. "He's nothing but a little blood-sucking whore moving from one bed to the next."

"Doesn't matter." Matt cocked his head so he could see Harley, giving the kneeling vampire a slow, appreciative head-to-toe glance. Then he locked stares with the assassin again and firmly stated, "He lays in a Lycan bed now."

The vampire sniffed the air, then shot a murderous look at Harley, his voice outraged and disbelieving. "You joined with a Lycan? Are you out of your mind?"

Wanting to deny it for appearances sake in front of Matt, but knowing it was the truth, Harley clamped his mouth shut and kept it that way. He was still having trouble shaking off the last of his death sleep to be all that coherent anyway. At least he could blame it on that.

In the answering silence, the vampire's startled gaze continued to whip from Matt to Harley and back again. "You took a vampire as a mate? He's an abomination! Diseased. Defective."

Matt shook his head. "He will heal in time."

"For all the good it will do him." The vampire snorted and fingered the useless weapon in his hands. "There is a death mark on him now."

"Then see that it's removed." The werewolf gave a pointed glance at the dust on the floor that was all that remained of the other Eliminator. "Or those that try to collect on it again will meet the same end as your companion did."

To Harley, Matt seemed to grow larger and more ferocious with every growled and snarled sentence. "My pack mates will rise up to meet the challenge if my mate continues to be hunted. Go back and tell your kind that."

He snapped at the vampire again, ripping a small wound in the assassin's his right cheek. The vampire flinched but didn't pull away. Matt tasted the blood, licking his lips as it dripped from his snout. "And if you return, I won't be this generous a second time." He snapped at the air in front of the vampire.

This time the Eliminator jerked his head back a scant inch in anticipation of a bite that didn't come. He snarled and yanked the empty crossbow up, the frustrated expression on his face revealing how much he wished it had another arrow in it. Even so, he remained as if rooted to the spot, nothing to do, but unable to leave.

Something about the vampire's rigid stance told Harley the vampire wasn't remaining still by choice. He watched Matt circle the ring of blue symbols, snarling and occasionally snapping at the unmoving vampire, taunting him like a wolf circled and harassed its prey before the kill.

Harley wasn't sure how, but in a shimmering instance Matt changed from werewolf to man. Human, naked and weaponless, he was still almost as large and intimidating as he had been as Lycan. He swept an arm outward and commanded, "Leave. While you still can."

The Eliminator looked up at the opening he had jumped through fifteen feet above him. He flicked a disgruntled glance at Harley then gave Matt a steely glare. "You'll heal him?"

Completely unaffected by his naked state, Matt moved to stand by the end of the bed, in front of Harley, blocking him from the other's hard stare. "He's already better. You saw that for yourself. He'll be strong again."

"But not completely normal." It wasn't a question.

"He's a vampire. What's normal about that to begin with?"

The Eliminator's glare hardened, but he remained silent. Springing to the balls of his feet, he jumped though the broken skylight and disappeared as suddenly as he had arrived.

Matt moved to a wall switch and hit a button. The buzz of a motor faintly filled the sudden stillness as a metal cover slid over the skylight blocking out the moon and stars. Once it was sealed he moved to the edge of the bed and pulled Harley to him, tangled sheets and all.

Surprising himself by melting into Matt's embrace, Harley grabbed hold of the man's thick biceps and tilted his head back to look him in the eye. "Why didn't he fight back?"

"He couldn't." He jerked his head toward the matching circles of blue paintings on the floor and ceiling. "The magic of the ring kept him contained."

"Magic?" The insistent, warm arms encircling him tightened. Harley felt a rush of desire shiver through him, stiffening his already hard cock. Danger tended to do that to him. The fact that Matt had been sporting a hard on during most of the action hadn't escaped his notice either. Now he had time to appreciate it and pay attention to it. He slipped a thigh between Matt's knees and wriggled his hips just a little. Matt's sharp look and hungry stare was enough to encourage him.

"Lycan and Vampyre societies have been at odds for centuries. You know that." Matt kissed the tip of Harley's nose, one hand slipping down to knead Harley's ass. "It's an ancient spell. It protects those within its boundaries from vampires. They can't cross it."

"Bullshit. I crossed it." He grunted as Matt lifted him off the bed and moved him backward, crawling onto the bed.

"You belong here." Carrying Harley, Matt walked on his knees to the center of the nest of blankets.

"So you keep saying."

"You will, too, soon enough." Matt swooped down and claimed Harley's lips, ravaging his mouth, battling his tongue and sending another electric shock of want and desire through the vampire's core.

By the time Matt released him, Harley swore even his dead soul took notice of the fiery passion that kiss ignited. It was as exciting as it was unnatural for the vampire. "So, is magic how you plan on keeping me here?"

Pushing Harley backward, Matt flopped them both down on the bed. "Only if you consider love, loyalty and desire for my mate to be magic."

His hand found Harley's cock and began to examine it in great, loving detail. He gripped both their cocks together in one hand began to pump them in a slow, seductive rhythm as he licked and kissed a random pattern over Harley's neck and chest.

His touch renewed Harley's interest in foreplay until panic and reason asserted themselves. "Stop that." He tried to nudge Matt's head up with his chin. "I'm not your mate." His hips rose up to meet Matt's on their own despite his strained words. "Are you crazy?" He panted through a sudden rush of desire that surged up his cock and buried itself in his belly, shaft harder and more eager in no time, teased to complete fullness by Matt's hard cock and knowing grip. "Vampire here, remember, asshole?" Harley snapped at Matt's chin, missing when Matt arched out of his reach. The movement pulled Matt's head back and shoved his groin down harder onto Harley's. Harley gave a groan of pleasure.

Chuckling, Matt dove down and quickly claimed Harley's mouth in a fast, hard kiss again, then pulled back far enough to stare into Harley's eyes. His gaze flickered down to the fangs and back to recapture Harley's softening glare. "Kind of hard to forget right now." He winked and smiled. "But it doesn't change anything. You're mine. Named, mated, fought for, won and claimed already."

"So what's that?" He gave an indelicate snort. "The werewolf version of 'signed, sealed and delivered'? I get a leash and collar to go with it?"

"Something like that." Laughing out loud this time, Matt eased both of their arms up the bed until Harley's wrists were pinned down by his neck. Matt released his hold then slid his fingers up to lace with Harley's unresisting ones. When he met no complaints, he locked their hands together. "After all, you were sent to me. To keep safe."

"What? Who? No one sent me anywhere." The disbelief dripped off his words. Harley snorted and lowered his gaze. The seductive thrusts against his groin stopped and the sudden loss of intimacy made him feel empty. "No one cares enough to send me anywhere 'safe'."

"My uncle and my mom cared." Matt's free hand gently forced Harley's chin up until they could see eye to eye. "They sent you here."

"Bullshit." Harley tried to pull away but Matt refused to let go. Harley had to blink to clear the sudden blurring in his vision. "You're nuts." He wanted to believe Matt, but it didn't make sense. "I don't know any werewolves!" A small, self-deprecating chuckle escaped him as he added, "And I sure don't know your mom."

"Sure you do." Matt's smiled widened. He sniffed Harley's cheek. "She touched your cheek," he nuzzled Harley's face, then planted his nose on Harley's nearby left hand, "and your hand. I smelled her on you right off. Why do you think I came over and talked to you in the bar?" He sniffed at Harley's right hand. "Uncle Abe shook your hand, too."

Slack jawed, Harley found himself almost speechless. "That PIA trucker is your uncle? I rode all the way here with a werewolf and didn't know it?" Disconcerted, a deep frown marred his face. "Christ, I am fucked up."

"Yep." Matt bussed a quick kiss on the frown and rolled a little to one side to get a better grip on their cocks. His hand never faltered in the smooth, slip-sliding rhythm that had Harley arching up into his hold. "And he delivered you, all wrapped up in a yellow ribbon."

The satin feel of flesh on flesh pushed his lusts higher. The rush of pleasure was so intense he almost missed the rest of what Matt was saying. "What? What ribbon?" He blinked and remembered the only thing he had worn that was yellow. "That old coat that lady at the cafe gave me?"

Matt smirked. "My old parka my mom gave you."

"Christ!"

"No, werewolf."

"Asshole." Harley search for a more derogatory term but all he could work up any feeling for was a lame taunt. He found his heart wasn't willing to help him abuse his new lover. "Beast."

"Corpse."

Eyes narrowed, Harley arched into Matt's fist as the man purposely sped up his strokes, making it nearly impossible for Harley to talk without moaning. "Carnivore."

"Cadaver."

"Ah! That was a low blow." It was hard not to groan

on the last word.

"No, but this is." Matt slid down Harley's body and took the head of his cock into his mouth. He sucked until his cheeks hollowed out, flicking the slit at the tip with his stiffened tongue.

"Fuck!" Harley thrust his hips upward, but Matt's large hands found his hips and anchored him back down to the bed. Another fierce suck and tongue probe, then Matt released him, sliding back up to lick and bite each of his swollen nipples. He dragged his teeth over their peaks until Harley hissed and grabbed the back of his head, crushing his face to the vampire's chest. "Mother fuck!"

Pulling away, Matt blew a stream of warm air over one wet, chilled tit, fingering it as it crinkled and hardened. "Hey, leave my mom out of our bed."

"Christ, you didn't have any problem thinking about her before when we fucked." Harley tried to draw Matt's face back down and Matt obliged long enough to suckle the other tit for a brief second before repeating the tweak and blow game.

"That was different. She marked you for me to find. Her scent will be gone soon. Replaced with mine." Matt began kissing his way down Harley's chest to his belly, mapping each rib and curve of the vampire's torso with his lips and tongue.

Harley snorted and gasped, threading his fingers in Matt's hair, body too focused on the sensations he was experiencing and the return of his blood lust to care about the implied ownership. Besides, he was beginning to like the idea of belonging to Matt, with Matt.

His protest came out much weaker than he had planned. "Peed on me like a tree stump?"

"No." Matt surged up and nuzzled at Harley's sensitive neck then blew in his ear as he whispered, "I filled you full of my load and didn't pull out until it invaded your body and found your undead soul. Then I invaded that, too."

He bit down on the carotid artery in Harley's neck and the vampire bucked up, writhing and swearing. "Why you sweet-talker, you. Charmed me through my ass, did you?"

"Right up your ass, sweetheart." Matt raked his teeth across Harley's skin, leaving a red trail that led from his neck to his groin.

Pulling Matt up by his hair until they were face to face again, Harley locked stares with the man. He let his well-practiced bravado fall away for the first time in three decades, allowing his true feelings to shine through his eyes and unguarded expression.

"Hey." He felt his lips quiver and his chest constrict, but Harley managed to get the words out. "Why don't you come and sweet-talk me some more." He swallowed hard but was encouraged by the gentle smile on Matt's lips. "Show me what this mating stuff is all about."

Soul Desire

The gentle grope at his leg was at once familiar and strange, the touch of an almost forgotten lover. But this caress was light and insistent, not the bold contact Mason was use to nudging at him in the middle of the night. Eric's demanding wake-up calls had always been smooth and heavy, full of need and passion. This fluttering, insistent pull to his thigh was in the old familiar spot, but it felt wrong, foreign, as if a stranger was in bed with him. It wasn't like Eric, but then it couldn't be. Eric was dead.

"What...Who's there?"

Jerking awake with a start, Mason woke panting, heart thundering under his bare ribs, sheets clenched in his fists, a fine sheen of sweat making his pajama bottoms cling to his legs. His sleep blurred vision wavered a bleary focus, the deeper shadows in the corners of the room a pitch black, their edges reaching out like slender gray arms to embrace the other objects in the dark room.

"Is someone there?"

Mason squinted and brushed his bangs out of his eyes, a thin white haze blurring his sight more than usual for a few seconds. When still nothing in the room was recognizable, he fumbled for his glasses on the bedside table, knocking into the lamp and shoving a book he had been reading earlier to the floor.

Glasses on and eyes focusing in the shadowed gloom, Mason blinked several times to dispel what seemed like a cloud of fog hanging over the bottom of the bed. A puff of chill night air seeped under the small window he had propped open a crack before going to bed. The tiny gust barely ruffled the curtains but the fog disappeared so fast Mason doubted it was there to begun with. A few embers in the fireplace on the wall opposite his bed glowed to life briefly then faded out as the breeze did the same.

Heart still pounding, he took his glasses back off and tossed them on the stand, slipping under the thick down comforter as he did so. The first unnerving fight-or-flight response faded away as he lay back to the comfort of the thick pillow and warm blankets

His thigh tingled where he'd imagined the hand touching him and he rubbed over it, his fingers automatically sliding to his groin to fondle his sudden erection. He always got hard when he was scared. Eric had loved watching horror movies with him naked on the couch. They rarely even got to see the end of the movie.

He worked his hand faster determined to get some pleasure from the disturbed sleep. His cock was hard as nails, but the mental stimulus wasn't cooperating. He gave up after a few minutes, having achieved nothing but an aching wrist and a sore, chaffed cock. Even conjuring up images of Eric hadn't helped.

The gloomy autumn weather here fit his mood and the barren sea cliffs and remote location made him feel secure and comfortable to be alone with his thoughts. Not that his thoughts were all that pleasant of late. He used to wonder if you could die from a broken heart if he should lend the process a hand and speed it up. He had been glad these fleeting thoughts hadn't lingered or intensified. They had scared him.

But now he had a new source to scare him—a haunted bedroom in a creaking old Maine estate. There wasn't any alcohol in the room, Mason hadn't had a drink in ages and yet he'd just caught a whiff of brandy on that faint, chilly draft.

§ § §

Rolling over to glance at the bedside clock, Mason grimaced at the bright red numbers.

"7:10. Shit."

Sitting up on the edge of the bed, he stared at the erection tenting his pajama bottom. "Lot of fucking good you do for me. Numb bastard. All you're good for is aggravating my carpal tunnel." With a flick of his fingers he thwacked his cock, then yelped when a bolt of pain punched his groin. "Fuck! I guess you're not so numb after all." He rubbed at his sore dick with one hand and his grit-filled eyes with his other.

Deciding an unfamiliar bathroom would best be appreciated if he could actually see it, he grabbed his glasses off the bedside stand and stumbled to find the toilet. Contact lenses could wait until after he had showered. Right now he needed hot water and, possibly, once he more awake, he might give a handful of soap and a tight grip a try to ease his erection enough to take a piss.

Steam billowed around Mason and rolled over the top of the shower door. The water pressure was delightfully strong for an old inn. Thick torrents of stinging hot water pounded over his tingling skin, turning it a bright pink. The pulsing beat of the shower spray worked the tension out of his neck and loosened his lower back. Travel always made his back ache. Cramped airline seats, taxis with no shocks, and strange beds all added up to headaches and tight shoulders for Mason -- although he had to admit his bed had been pretty comfortable for an off-the-beaten-path hotel. Not too hard, and the covers smelt fresh and clean like they had been hung outside on a clothesline. The pillows had been plump, and there were actually more of them than he needed. The whole inn was shaping up to be more pleasurable than he had expected.

With pleasure on his mind, Mason lathered up his hands and blindly set the bar of soap aside. Turning his back to the spray, he ran both lathered palms down his belly and let them wander in the nest of dark hair surrounding his cock. His dick was still hard with his morning erection and his bladder strained a little with the need for release.

He slid his cock through his soapy fist and used his other hand to fondle and tug his balls. His flesh was willing but his mind didn't seem to want to cooperate yet. He stroked and rubbed, fingering his scrotum and even easing a finger tip into his tight, long unused hole, but nothing helped pushed the faint pleasant sensation over the edge toward a more satisfying, needed climax.

Tired of the lonely, unhappy numbness that had invaded his life and his body, Mason forced himself to relax back against the shower wall. He tried to conjure up a hot, erotic vision. Nothing came immediately to mind so he concentrated on the smooth, icy tiles pressed to his back and ass.

Hot water pummeled his chest and splashed down his thighs in tickling rivers. The steam filled the small cubicle and the air grew heavy, invading his lungs and penetrating his skin. Mason's breathing slowed. He closed his eyes and let his mind drift with the mist. Gradually, the hand delivering pleasurable strokes along his cock seemed to belong to someone else. The grip was tighter, the rhythm smooth, but with a little twist on the downward stroke that made him gasp and rock his hips into the beat. His other hand caressed his sac, a gentle pull and rolling motion that reached deep to the root of his cock. He hadn't slipped his hand near his opening, but it felt like a fingertip had entered him, just a little. He guessed it was the unfamiliar rhythm of strokes he was using -- and that fact it had been months since he'd spent more than three minutes trying to bring himself off. The sensations almost seemed new, he thought.

Without conscious effort, he found the slip-slide of soapy hand over slick, hard flesh increase. Sensation bombarded Mason as his climax built. Assaulting his sense and heightening his pleasure, his skin was alive with an almost electric sizzle. He was sure he heard the shower water hiss as it struck him. Even the fantasy seemed to become real. Although his back was plastered to the wall, the area under one shoulder stayed cool. But, the air seemed heavier and hotter on his neck just above the cold spot -- almost like someone had a hand on his neck, standing next to him, breathing on his wet skin.

Mason's eyes flew open and he glanced around, his blurred vision seeing nothing but foggy white while his mind chastised him for giving in to foolish, childish scares.

Mason shook of the sensation he wasn't alone and concentrated on recapturing the erotic sizzle that had dampened with the scared rush of adrenaline. His mind drifted imagining a new lover, someone so different from Eric that his mind couldn't possibly confuse them. Someone dark, tall and ruggedly handsome someone who had strong hands and didn't mind a short-sighted, artistic geek with so much emotional baggage he'd considered hiring a porter just to carry it around.

One more rough tug that Mason felt all the way up his gut made his hole clench and his eyes water, and he was suddenly coming. Thin ropes of cum blended with the soapsuds and disappeared down the drain with the shower spray. Mason wrung the last of the orgasm out of his body and sagged against the wall. He hadn't climaxed in so long he'd forgotten how limp his knees and his cock got afterward. He rubbed at the cool spot that lingered on his shoulder, vaguely disturbed by the chill that settled in the hot space.

Once his cock went soft, he relieved his bladder, aiming for the drain with as much accuracy as his eyesight allowed him, then set about getting his morning routine underway.

No matter how comfortable the inn was, this was still

a strange shower and bath. Without his glasses on or his contacts in, Mason had to fumble around to find things. The shampoo he'd brought with him was a blur in the shower, identified only by the shape of the clear bottle and the greenish-blue color of the soap inside. His bar of white handsoap melted into the white shower surround, and he had run his hands over the built-in shelves to find it every time he set it down. Thank God the hot and cold taps were always on the same sides.

Reluctantly turning off the flood of soothing, liquid heat, Mason slid the door open and stepped out into the unfamiliar bathroom.

"Fuck!"

Misjudging the height, he hit his foot on the shower lip, but managed to steady himself with a hand on the nearby sink. He was surrounded by clouds of thick white steam billowing out of the open shower and hanging like storm clouds over his head. In a few seconds they thinned but a band of mist seemed to hang in front of him so dense that his senses lied to him, telling him he could reach out and touch it. Instead, Mason grabbed one of the thick fluffy towels off the heating bar and wrapped it around his waist.

Moving to the sink, he walked right through the dense bar of mist, dissipating it. The movement stirred a breeze and a chill ran down his spine as his pink skin cooled. He shook off the shiver, finger combed his hair out of his eyes with one hand, and grabbed for his toothbrush with the other.

All around him the strange little room was shrouded

in a white mist that he couldn't seem to dispel. The room felt too close and the air too heavy suddenly. Despite the thickness of the steam, Mason had the impression he was being watched, but a quick glance around showed him he was alone in the small bathroom.

He shrugged off the concern and bent over the sink to brush his teeth. With a quick rinse and spit, Mason straightened and looked into the mirror to check the condition of his morning stumble. Even at twenty-eight, he only needed to shave every other day if he wasn't working.

A quick glance into the mirror sent a new chill across Mason's overly flushed skin. In the glass, over his left shoulder, was what looked like a man's face. It was indistinct, like the face of the Man in the Moon, more caters, ridges and shadows than real features, but a face nonetheless, a pale smear of white and gray that stared back at him in the silvered glass. Even without his glasses, he knew facial features when he saw them.

Mason gripped the sink's edge with both hands as his breath caught in his throat. He could feel his heart hammering under his ribcage. Despite the humidity and heat trapped in the small room, a sheen of cold sweat broke out over his entire body and his lips went numb. Eyes locked on the unmoving face, he slowly reached out and tried to rub it off the mirror as if it were just steam on the glass. When it didn't budge, he lowered his gaze and slowly turned his head to look over his shoulder. There was nothing behind him.

Mason jumped and spun around, arms batting at the remnants of mist in the room. Once the steam had dissolved into the far corners and his heartbeat has returned to something close to normal, Mason turned back around and cautiously let his gaze dart to the mirror. With one hand, he rubbed at the surface with the hand towel, while he divided his attention between the glass and the room behind him.

Deciding against a shave, he left the bathroom, still wearing his towel, hair sopping wet and bangs in his eyes. He shivered at the coolness of the bedroom, but he had no intention of returning to the bath.

Dropping onto the edge of the bed, Mason slapped his glasses onto his face with a bit more force than was really necessary. He sat shivering and watching the steam drift out of the bathroom.

§ § §

Dressed in jeans, untied hiking boots, and a soft, beige pullover sweater, Mason decided to forget the contacts and stick with his glasses. They were horn-rimmed and geeky, but more comfortable than his lenses. He was here to relax. There was no one to impress or who gave a care about what he looked like anymore. So far, he'd met only one older woman who had manned the registration desk. Very nice, but not his type.

Running both hands through his overly long, dark wavy hair, he checked his pants pockets to make sure he'd transferred everything from one pair of pants to the next and headed out the door to find breakfast. He didn't have much of an appetite anymore, but he guessed it had been roughly twenty hours since he'd eaten anything that could remotely be described as nourishing.

It had to be the dim lighting in this old place. The pale, pinched face that looked back at him from the bathroom mirror this morning suggested he had better start taking better care of himself and soon. His peridot green eyes made the pallor all the more alarming, especially when framed by his dark, now collar-length hair.

Making time for eating or haircuts had been less of a priority over these last few months. It wasn't one now, but Mason didn't like the idea of fainting from malnourishment while in the company of strangers. He was geeky, small and slender, barely five-foot-seven and stretching to make the one-fifty mark, but he hated people thinking he was delicate or fragile. Emotionally numb best described him at present, but he wasn't delicate.

He checked that the window was still open just a crack, cast am admiring looking around the spacious room decorated in comforting shades of light and dark blue. The furniture was dark cherry, sturdy with a four-poster bed and matching ornate side tables, dresser and armoire. The table lamp he'd almost knocked over during the night has a shade of jewel-tone stained glass in a dragonfly design. By the fireplace were two low overstuffed plaid chairs that shared an ottoman. A thick chenille throw was draped over the back of one chair. It was a cozy room made for a man, but with a light touch that kept it from being too overly masculine. Mason decided it would suit him well over the next few weeks. Storm Inn. It was a great name. Mason thought it suited him. His life felt like a building storm, disheveled and wind torn, with torrents of tears that fell like rainy downpours. Even the thunderous outbursts of rage ripped by jolts of lightning hot pain came without warning sometimes, startling even him. It seemed as if Mason was losing control over his emotions and his life. Storm Inn sounded perfect for him.

It even looked perfect when he checked in last evening. The leaded glass windows only let scattered sunlight it, muting it to soft shades of dark blues and green. The yellow, brown, blue and beige paint on the clapboard exterior, though in good repair and recently painted, looked weather-weary and dull. Barren trees surrounded the house on all sides with a forest of pines a few hundred feet back around three sides of the perimeter.

The main lobby was thick with oriental rugs and dark cheery furniture. Wine and sapphire blue over-stuffed cottage chairs and loveseats spread out over the huge area, crammed into corners and nooks around the space. A massive fieldstone fireplace dominated the room and several deep, cushioned chairs were drawn up close and cozy to it. Mason looked forward to spending time there in the evenings.

At the top of wide-open staircase that ran up the very center of the inn, Mason paused to scan the organized clutter of the lobby. It contained the ancient, dark oak registration counter and mailboxes on one side, but the majority of the room was the cozy salon. A fire already blazed on the hearth, pushing back the early morning fall chill.

Mason shrugged his shoulders against the chill and charged down the stairs, gaze wandering from corner to corner, looking of the woman he'd met the night before.

"Hello? Ruby?"

Looking behind the desk, he found no evidence of another person, but the fire and the steaming cup of coffee on a stand beside a fireplace chair told him he wasn't the first one awake.

"Hello? Anybody around? Ruby?"

A snap and thud yanked his attention to the fire. A log had toppled off the fire grate and rolled precariously near the edge of the stone hearth, just a few inches from the carpet. Mason hurried to the raised stone, grabbed a poker from the stand and awkwardly struggled with the crumbling log as it shattered in a shower of hot rolling embers. He'd never worked with a real fire. His apartment in NYC only had a gas fireplace for looks. He batted at the largest of the chunks with the poker but only managed to send a shower of sparks up to land on his inner thighs, exposed as he crouched.

"Shit!" Mason jumped back, ash-tipped poker flailing in the air. He stumbled on the edge of the oriental rug, his untied boot slipping part way off and tripping him all the more. One hand batted out the sparks on his jeans as he lost his balance and landed on his ass hard enough to jar his glasses askew, back shoved against a heavy wine-colored ottoman and matching chair. A new ember tumbled from the fire. Instinctively, he jumped forward and reached for it with his bare hand.

Suddenly Mason was lifted back from behind by a steel band that scooped him up around his waist. He was molded against a hard chest, his ass comfortably tucked into the crook of a thick, bent thigh. The wildly waving poker was plucked from his hand. A deep voice chuckled softly in his ear.

"Hold up there, torch. You're going to set yourself on fire *and* poke someone's eye out at the same time."

Panicked, Mason fought the restrictive hold until the man spoke, the warm, amused voice sending shivers of another kind down his back. Mason twisted around in surprise, as the hands on his waist became more of a steadying hold than a restraining grip. His body hadn't responded like that to another male voice in a long, long time.

Nose barely inches away from a square jaw, Mason looked up into a face that made him automatically reach up to push his crooked glasses back into place to make sure he was seeing things correctly. He got a swift glance at dark, cheerful eyes, at dark hair and broad cheekbones, together composing a very handsome face. Then, the steel arms heaved him into the ottoman beside the hearth chair and out of the secure embrace.

The man moved closer to the fire, exchanged the useless poker for long-handled shovel. He expertly scooped up the spattered, glowing coals and dumped them back into the crackling fire. It took him about ten seconds.

"Not much good around open flames, are you?" It was said with a grin and a wink so captivating Mason couldn't work up the steam to be mad. He sighed and picked at a tiny scorch spot on the leg of his jeans, trying hard not to gaze for too long into the stranger's dark eyes. He felt the man watching his every move, assessing him. He reached down and tugged his boot back into place.

"Not much, no. I opted out of the Boy Scouts." He inexplicably wished he'd taken the time to put his contacts in after all. Mason shoved at the bridge of his glasses then readjusted them when they moved too snuggly against his face. "I got picked on enough for being smaller than the rest of the guys at school. I didn't think joining a group that concentrated on developing he-man skills was a great way to avoid more of the same."

The man chuckled again, the sound warm and rich. It made something unfurl in Mason's belly, deep down in the pit of stomach.

"I think they teach a few more things that he-man skills, but it's just a guess. Didn't have them where I grew up." He sat down on the edge of the chair closely facing Mason's seat and stuck out his hand. "Hi, I'm Eli, by the way."

"Mason Everett." Mason clasped the callused palm and watched his own hand disappear in the mighty grip. The heat from Eli's palm was intense. Mason actually thought his own would come away reddened, but his hand only tingled and his fingers twitched. He rubbed them on his jeans to lessen the sensation. Then, to stop his own gaze from lingering too long on the man, he glanced around the sitting room. Eli's charming smile might be catching, and it won't do to be chipper this early in the morning on a day he had promised himself he'd sleep in and hadn't.

"I was looking for Ruby. Is she the housekeeper? I thought she could tell me where to find breakfast."

A fifty-something, cheery woman with smooth skin

and gray-streaked hair held in a loose bun by antique bone sticks had registered him on his arrival late last evening. She had chattered non-stop once she shook his hand in greeting, her own grip firm and lingering just a little longer than Mason had expected. By the time she had shown him his room, he'd realized that Ruby punctuated her gentle and reassuring presence with small touches and fluttering pats.

Ruby made him think of an old maiden relative, Aunt Sophie, the one everyone whispered was slightly off, but whose appreciation and lectures about art had inspired mason to try his hand at it. He never told her before she passed on, but she had put him on his career path. Slightly off her rocker or not, he had a soft spot for Aunt Sophie that colored his assessment of Ruby. Mason had instantly liked her, especially when she had told him breakfast was served until 10:00 a.m.

"Kitchen's that way. We're going to be informal here for the next week or two." Eli pointed to an archway to their left. "No one else works here at the moment. Maid service comes in from town once a week." He gave Mason a thoughtful, appraising stare. "Not usually many visitors this time of year. The leaves are gone and the snow hasn't come yet. Too cold and dreary for most people."

Eli hadn't pried, just left the door open for discussion if Mason wanted to elaborate on why he'd isolated himself out there.

But Mason wasn't in the mood to talk about it yet. He switched to a more neutral subject.

"But...there was a Ruby here last night when I arrived."

Mason knew he had been tired but he didn't think he'd been hallucinating, as well. "She checked me in. She was a little eccentric, but I didn't think she'd walked in off the street. Kind of hard to do that way out here anyway. I'd assumed she worked here, owned the inn maybe." He shrugged his shoulders, glanced around the comfortable, warm sitting room and shyly added, "The place has a homey feel to it, like a woman's touch. My apartment doesn't have that."

Eli smiled and gave a pleased chuckle. "Thanks. I'll take that as a compliment. My mother did all of the decorating before her death a while back. I've kept it pretty much the same since then. She had good taste." Eli ran one of his palms over the fabric of the chair he was sitting on. Mason found himself wishing it was his skin under the hand instead. The thought startled him and he jumped when Eli's smooth, deep voice spoke again. "Ruby's just a friend. I had a town board meeting last night and couldn't be here myself. So she filled in. I should have given you my last name earlier. I'm the innkeeper. Eli Storm."

Mason's eyes betrayed him. Faced with seeing this man everyday for several weeks was going to be a challenge. Besides good looking, Eli was intelligent and hard working. This cozy, well-maintained inn showed that. Just his luck, Eli was turning out to be a nice guy as well.

His gaze flickered over Eli's features and he swallowed past a dry throat. He hadn't been interested in another man for so long he forgotten how it made him flush. Dating had always been difficult for him and now a twinge of guilt choked off the pleasant feeling of attraction.

"She was nice. I'd hope to see her again. She kind of

looked familiar to me." He shrugged again and readjusted his glasses. "Must be because she reminds me of someone I used to know."

"You'll see her. She stops by a lot, especially during the slow season. Until next week, you're the only guest staying here." Eli leaned closer and said in an amused, conspiratorial whisper, "She doesn't think I should be alone in a haunted house."

"What? Haunted? You're kidding me, right?"

Mason knew his eyes had gone wide behind his glasses by the way Eli's gaze was drawn to them. Eric had always said his glasses looked dorky, but they made his eyes appear bigger and their crystal green color hypnotizing. He tried to squint to counteract it, hoping Eli didn't think he was flirting with him. Even if his body was telling him he was attracted to the man, he wasn't ready for anything, including harmless flirting. He thought he'd seen a look of interest on the guy's face earlier, but he couldn't be sure. He didn't think it was a good idea to explore it. He'd just keep his newfound fascination with the innkeeper confined to his daydreams.

"You don't actually believe in that, do you?" Mason couldn't help glancing around the room. It still held the gray edges of morning light. He could tell it was going to be a dreary, dark day. *Perfect for introspection. And ghost stories.* He shifted a bit closer to the fire and tugged his sweater sleeves down to the tips of his fingers. "Ghosts? Who is it?"

"Reported to be my great-grandfather, Eugene Storm. The man that built this house." Eli glanced around the room, too, but Mason couldn't tell if it was more for effect than an effort to find anything otherworldly. "Never seen anything to completely convince me of it."

"Not *completely*?"

Eli tilted his head to one side and shrugged, his dark eyebrows raised and then lowered once, very quickly. The smile dimmed a little, but a sparkle of mischief shone in his eyes. "No, not completely."

"Give! What?"

"Not much. Maybe a shimmer of white out of the corner of my eye, or wind that seems to call my name on the cliffs, but I'm told I'm not very sensitive to the paranormal vibes. Too practical and closed-minded." He smiled wider. "For a gay man, I rate low on the touchy-feely meter."

Heart beating a little faster at that last revelation, Mason pretended not to let Eli's sexual orientation register as important to him. Not quite knowing how to read the other man, Mason narrowed his eyes and persisted.

"But *Ruby* believes the house is haunted?" He jumped slightly when his stomach suddenly rumbled, adding a disembodied growl to the gloomy conversation. He placed a sweater sleeve-covered hand on his stomach and cast an embarrassed grimace at Eli. "Sorry. No ghosts or goblins, just me. It's been a long time since lunch yesterday."

"Yes, Ruby believes in ghosts but she calls them spirits." Smile still intact, Eli shook his head and stood. "She also believes in three meals a day, starting with breakfast."

His tone was brisk and crisp, making the whole room

seem less dark and eerie to Mason. Eli's voice had a power to it that made it a one-man PA system if he pitched it just right. It made Mason's stomach flutter like the drums in the marching bands did.

"I've only made coffee so far. Why don't you join me in the kitchen and I'll make us both something. Like pumpkin pancakes and sausage?"

"Pumpkin pancakes? Ah...Do you have any cereal?"

§ § §

The walk to the cliffs only took about ten minutes. The path was winding and long so Mason decided to take a more direct route up the hill through rock and scrub grass. The grass grew in clumps so thick and raveled that it nearly tripped Mason on several occasions. He stopped after the first twenty feet to ties his boots tighter. At home he preferred sneakers. The hiking boots he packed for the wilds of northern Maine were heavy and restrictive. He always wore them loosely tied, but he could see it being hazardous to his health. He'd have to remember to take the time to tie them properly.

He persisted in taking his makeshift route, but by the time he reached the point Eli had described over breakfast as having the best view of the ocean, Mason was panting and his thighs burned. City walking and apartment elevators hadn't prepared him for hiking up a rugged hilltop.

At the edge of the narrow cliff, Mason threw himself down on the ground. He lay back to watch the gray clouds gathering while he caught his breath again. They didn't move with any real speed, but they were growing in number and density. The air was heavy with moisture, scented by grass and the ocean. His sweater and jeans had become damp to the touch. The sand and grass under him molded to his body and stayed that way, firmly packed.

It was peaceful, if a little storm-swept. Mason rolled over onto his belly and wiggled closer to the edge so he could see both the blue-green ocean and the gray sky.

Breathing back to normal, Mason propped his chin on his hands and listened to the sound of the water and wind mixed with the occasional sea gull cry and the faint rustling of the tall grasses around him. He couldn't hear the waves breaking against the bottom of the cliff from this position, but he saw them in his mind, crashing on the rocks below, beating uselessly against an unyielding surface.

It reminded him of his pain over Eric's death. He felt as if he was riding a wave, always trying to reach the safety of dry, stable land, but the rocks, like the harshness of Eric's death, constantly loomed in his way, forcing him back into the water, back into the cold, pointless hollow his life had become.

He hadn't meet anyone new he was interested enough in to consider getting to know better. That is, if he didn't count the new innkeeper. Eli Storm had definitely made his cock sit up and take notice. Eli did funny things to his stomach, too.

And, here he was -- lying in wet scrub grass on the edge of a tall cliff in dreary Maine, listening to the ocean, watching the storm clouds gather and getting sand in his underwear and hair.

A particularly dark cloud pushed its way into the gray gathering overhead and Mason decided if he was going to get a look at the rocks below it was now or never. The wind was whipping his hair in his eyes and the air had a biting sting to its chill.

He crawled the last few feet to the edge of the cliff and poked his head out over the drop. The huge, white rocks along the shoreline stood up out of the whirling, foam-peaked waters. They were battered and dowsed by waves of frothy white that left behind shallow black pools on their pitted and worn surfaces. There were hundreds of them all along the cliff's edge where rugged land met unyielding ocean. It made Mason dizzy to look at them.

"Whoa! Where's a guard rail when you need one?"

His voice was lost in the wind. Mason propelled himself backward on his belly for a couple yards before standing up. He didn't mind heights, but the spongy wet sand and earth under him didn't fill him with confidence that close to the edge.

Once on his feet, he realized just how much sand had made its way into his boots and clothing. He shook out his sweater, dusted off the outside of his jeans, wiggled and shook his butt trying to dislodge sand from inside his pants, and then looked for a clean, dry place to sit down to work off his boots.

Several feet away a six-foot long outcropping of earth and rocks jutted up from the otherwise unbroken plateau. The rocks were white and worn smooth on the surfaces, like the shoreline rocks below. Someone had carried them up from the base of the cliffs, rescuing each one from the punishing ocean waters.

The largest stone was long and thin, almost like a park bench. Mason sat on it, shivering at the cold that immediately seeped into his bones through his damp jeans. Moving with as much haste as he could with cold, numb fingers, he worked loose the leather ties on his ankle-high boots and shook each one out. He was brushing the last of the clinging sand from his sock when a hand pushed at his back, nudging him forward. He lost the grip on his boot. It tumbled to the sandy grass.

"What the hell?"

Mason jumped and twisted around, surprised he wasn't alone. Then… astonished that he *was* alone. There was no one at his back. He spun around on the rock and checked in all direction, but only a lone seagull flew overhead. There was no other living soul near him nor could one have advanced on him without his knowing unless the route had been over the cliff's edge, and he knew that was impossible. The beach had been deserted when he had looked down only a few moments ago.

The cold, building wind whipped his too-long bangs into his eyes, catching them on his glasses, and blinding him until he swiped them out of the way with an impatient hand. Heart pounding from the momentary fright, Mason glanced around one more time, convinced himself it had just been the wind or his imagination and sat back down to retrieve his boot.

He spread his legs to reach down between them to

grab his boot, tugged its heavy leather back into place and tied it in record time. Still bent low working the ties, a dark shadow passed over him and he jerked his face upward.

He laughed out loud, a nervous, out of place sound, as he realized he had overreacted to a pair of snowy egrets as they flew by, low and large.

So much for this calming nature shit. A soul-searching, solitary walk on the cliffs is not as relaxing as the movies lead everyone to believe. I need to get a grip.

Closing his eyes, Mason took a deep breath and slowly let it out. He squared his shoulders and let his chin drop to his chest, attempting a relaxation technique a yoga instructor had shown him once. The tension eased from his back a bit, and he felt his arms loosen up slightly. The wind became irregular, a siren's song, lulling him into a calmer state.

A tingling pressure blossomed at the back of his neck, the spot that always felt so good when Eric rubbed it after Mason had spent a long hard day hunched over his drawing table. Mason concentrated on the pressure, expecting it to spread down his back and travel through his body. But, no. The pressure didn't move, didn't slide down his body. Instead, it rested there, at his neck, growing colder, growing heavier. The visual of an ice bag popped into his mind, then morphed into the image of a bloody, refrigerated dinner steak lying on his neck before turning into the white, icy, cold hand of a dead man.

"Fuck!"

Leaping off the rock, Mason stumbled away from the outcropping, one hand massaging the back of his neck, trying to restore warmth into the cold flesh. His eyes frantically searched the empty land around him. He started to run without conscious thought.

By the time Mason was half way to the inn he had lectured himself twice on the need to focus on something beside death from now on. Death was the stronger conclusion. He'd even managed to remind himself that nut cases were rarely attractive as dating material. He had better put a stop to all the morbid thoughts and jumpy behavior if he had any interest whatsoever of finding out if Eli Storm was flirting with him in earnest or just for the hell of it. He was a little old to be influenced by ghost tales and haunted houses.

Wasn't he?

§ § §

Feeling the exhaustion lift a little each day, Mason spent the next week exploring the shoreline, reading books from the shelves in Eli's library, eating bits of the man's cooking and talking away his afternoons with a visiting Ruby like today.

"So why did you come here, Mason? Isolated Maine inns by the sea are great getaways for moody writers or love-struck couples, but not single young men. At least, not alone. What do you do for a living?" She smiled and slipped two fresh-from-the-oven cookies onto a plate in front of him.

"I work for a large advertising firm in New York City. I'm a graphics artist."

"Artist! Really? How interesting. Do you paint? I love watercolors."

"I can but in my work I create designs and art for advertising campaigns and fundraisers mostly. Big business lots of pressure, but I like being able to see my work on billboards." The smell of oatmeal, cinnamon and raisins filled the air. He could barely keep from touching them while they cooled. He had a fleeting memory of his mother baking cookies for him after school.

He returned her smile with a crooked one of his own, clasping his coffee mug tighter. "I thought the name of inn fit my state of mind. Storm Inn by the stormy sea." He chuckled but he could tell by the look on her face, Ruby wasn't buying the offhand explanation.

"Really? That's the only reason to travel all the way out here alone?"

He supposed he should feel offended by her gentle prying but kitchen was cozy warm from the oven and her cable-sweatered, smiling presence was comforting.

Maybe they were right when they said it was easier to talk to strangers about a problem than it was to talk to friends. The heavy earthenware coffee cup was solid in his hands, its heat seeped all the way to his chest, loosing the constricting band of numb ache that had held him its grip for so long. For the first time since Eric's death he felt free to talking about it. Here, in stormy Maine with a stranger who baked him cookies and believed in ghosts.

"Okay, that's not the only reason but it is one of the reasons I pick here." He picked up a cookie and broke of a small chunk, popping it into to his mouth to chew silently for a moment to have time to form his thoughts. It was new getting ready to say it out loud for the first time.

"What's the other reasons?"

Mason sighed and swallowed savoring the flavors of oatmeal and spices. "My boss, David. My work was slipping. I've had trouble concentrating. He said it was time to get my head on straight. Big believer in 'tough love'." Mason grimaced and gave a grunted half-laugh. "The man has teenagers." He sighed and shifted in his seat. "He said I couldn't mourn forever."

A deep frown marred Ruby's round face. "Did you lose someone, Mason?"

He nodded, made to sip his coffee than stopped. He needed to talk not more caffeine. "Two years ago." He stopped to clear his throat but the words came easier than he thought they would. "I was with Eric for eight years, since I got out of college. I was twenty-two. Eric was twenty-seven, established in his career, tired of the dating scene already and looking to settle down. I never got into the dating thing and we just kind of meshed. I was devastated when he was gone."

"You broke up?"

He shook his head and took a deep breath, letting the words flow out as he exhaled. They seemed take the numbness in his chest with them. "Eric fell asleep at the wheel one night after working late and when off the road. Hit a tree. They said he died on impact."

A soft, strong hand grasped his wrist. He instantly

tried to pull away but the fingers gently forced its way down to his hand. Ruby gripped his finger, while her thumb made soothing circles over the back of his hand. Tears sprung to Mason eyes when he realized how long it had been since someone had touched him like this, how long since he'd let anyone touch to comfort and hold him. God, he missed being touched.

He blinked back the tears that threatened to fall, then curled his fingers around Ruby's, loosely at first, just to feel the warm and strength in her grip. "I grieved when Eric died, experienced all the classic stages of grief from denial when the police had informed me they'd found Eric's body at the crash site all the way to righteous anger over his falling asleep at wheel."

"I even tried to mentally bargain with the 'powers that be' to let me wake up and have the whole ugly mess be just some twisted nightmare. But I didn't need to wake up and it didn't go away. By the end of the first year I'd stopped listening for Eric's key in the door in the evenings and stopped hearing his voice in crowded rooms or on the busy streets. He doesn't even visit in my dreams anymore."

"It's hard to let go sometimes, sweetie, but you're a young man. You need to get on with your life. Don't you think Eric would have wanted that for you? I'm sure he loved you that much, to want to see you happy even if he was gone."

"Yeah, he would." His throat tightened stopping his next sentence, the pressure in his chest forcing the tears sitting in the corners of his eyes to brim. He felt them run under his chin and drip off but he made no move to wipe them away. There wasn't any point, more followed. "I've felt like I was just going through the motions lately. It's scary. I'm not ready to stop living. I'm not cut out to be alone, I know that. I came here because this is someplace Eric would never have come. No memories here, no reminders ever time I turn around. I think I'm ready to get back to living again."

"Sounds to me like you need a little rest and maybe a distraction or two."

"A distraction?" Mason wiped at one cheek and popped a piece of cookie in his mouth, trying not to sniffle too loudly. "Yeah, I could use one of those. Got any suggestions?"

"What about Eli?" Ruby smiled and winked. "I think he's pretty distracting. How about you?"

Mason snorted in disbelief but his mind was asking him the same questions.

§ § §

While his nights were spent in restless dreams filled with white mists and cold caresses under the thick, down comforter, his evenings were spent wrapped in a lap quilt in front of the fireplace, chatting with Eli.

It didn't hurt any either that Eli did appear to be interested in him as more than a guest or friendly visitor. Either that or Mason really had forgotten all the signals and feelings associated with flirting. He had a fluttering in his stomach when he glanced up and found Eli looking at him with that affectionate, hungry look.

Eli was giving him that look right now. It was late afternoon and Ruby was sitting at his side. Suddenly, the comfortable sitting room and the flickering fire seemed unusually warm. Mason shifted in his seat and blushed at the amused wink Eli sent him when he noticed him squirm.

"You're not dating anyone right now?" Mason couldn't help it. He had to know if there was some guy off fishing for the last week who would pop up as soon as Mason decided to get serious about letting Eli get a little closer. The man was too good a catch not to have someone around.

"Not many gay men in this tiny village, Mason. Least not ones I have any interest in. I'd rather be alone than leave my home and the family's business to relocate in a more populated area." With another teasing wink and roguish smile, Eli claimed, "Good things come to those that wait." That hungry, wanting look hit his eyes again. "You're proof of that."

Feeling a heat rise to his cheeks, Mason flashed Ruby a sheepish look. Her wide smile and rolling eyes made him chuckle out loud, but a sudden rush of nerves made him changed the subject. "I thought I'd go see the cliff at dawn tomorrow. Get the full effect of it the way it was meant to be seen. Do you know what time that'll be at?"

He'd been experiencing an increasing and indefinable, almost eerie pull to the rocky, cold cliff.

"What's dawn got to do with it?" Even with a perplexed look on his face, Eli was handsome, his gaze gentle. "That whole cliff face is shrouded in mist that early. You won't see anything."

"I'm confused." Mason felt more on the spot than when Eli had been flirting with him. He hated feeling dumb. "I thought that would be the best time of day. You said it was called Morning Cliff."

A deep frown furrowed Eli's brow. He stared at Mason for a moment, then the frown vanished. He gave a small grunt that sounded like restrained laughter and shook his head. "Not m-o-r-n-i-n-g cliff, Mason. M-o-u-r-n-i-n-g. As in 'sorrow over a loss'. *Mourning Cliff.* It was kind of like a lover's leap a few decades back. More than one depressed, grief-stricken person has jumped off that cliff." He paused then confessed, "Hell, my own great-grandmother did it."

"Seriously? Why?" Mason stared into his cup, his fingers idly tipping the mug up and down just a little, making the liquid slosh from side to side, as if looking for the answer in the rich brown depths. "I mean, I can understand missing someone..." He had to take a deep breath to steady his voice, "...so much every part of your whole body *aches* from sheer loneliness." He closed his eyes and willed the tears he felt brimming behind his them to fade. "And I can see thinking death would be a quick escape..." Mason swallowed hard, thankful he had his glasses on. It made it harder for Eli and Ruby to see his face. "When every morning fills you with a kind of debilitating dread."

He opened his eyes, sniffed into the fist he rubbed over his nose and blinked over at both Eli and Ruby. "But getting smashed to bits on a graveyard of rock in a freezing ocean is kind of a harsh way to go, don't you think?" Suddenly self-conscious under Eli's silent, appraising stare, Mason pushed his glasses back up his nose and shrugged, grimacing at the mental picture he had just painted. "That's *gotta* be messy."

Wordlessly Ruby reached out and rubbed Mason's arm. Her touch was consoling and it lingered, the warmth of her hand radiating through his sweater and relaxing his tense muscles. He realized his cup had been shaking while he talked, but her soothing grip eased the strain in his trembling arm. Mason transferred the cup to his other hand and set it down on a nearby table, inexplicably loath to move his other arm from her reach. It was weird, but Ruby made him feel calmer and more *unscrambled* than he had in months. She was like Valium in human form. On the other hand, Eli excited him.

Glancing up, Mason's gaze meet Eli's and he felt a slight flush color his face. He wasn't embarrassed by Ruby's attention, but knowing he had almost cried in front this man was embarrassing. He mentally sighed and chalked up one more mess up on the negative side for him as potential dating material.

Christ, he really had forgotten how to do this. These last two years it had been acceptable to come across to other guys as a nerdy flake because he really hadn't wanted to date any of them, but now that he'd literally fallen into the arms of someone he *was* attracted to, he didn't have a chance of succeeding if this kept up. Hell, *he* wouldn't date a guy as screwed up as he was!

"I'll bet it was messy, but I wasn't born when it happened." Eli's smile eased a little of Mason's stress. "Heard plenty of stories about it over the years, but most were just gossip and rumor."

"Why'd she do it? Or shouldn't I ask?"

"I don't have a problem talking about it. In fact, it's part of the folklore about the inn being haunted."

"She's the ghost?" Mason started, thoughts of the misty face in the bathroom mirror jumping to his mind. It hadn't looked to him like a woman. *If* it had been anything at all. "I thought it was supposed to be your grandfather?"

"It is. Unusual things started happening about ten years ago, after we had a fire. The entire kitchen burnt, down to the basement. When we were rebuilding, we found a hidden wine cellar that had been sealed off from the rest of the house. Still had a number of wine bottles in it, too. Like it had been sealed off in a hurry. Good wine, too."

"That's kind of weird."

Eli shrugged, obviously at a loss for an explanation. "I had it opened back up and we use it for the inn. We serve dinner here twice a month and on holidays. It's been great to have a wine cellar in the place."

"And? Tell him, Eli." Ruby lightly smacked the man's broad shoulder. She turned to Mason and eagerly added, "This is where the story gets interesting again."

Rolling his eyes, Eli grudgingly acknowledged, "*And...* that's when things," he gestured to the empty air all around them, "started getting... *odd* around here."

Ruby nodded and rephrased Eli's meaning for Mason. "Hauntings."

"Happenings." Eli enunciated the word carefully and

gave Ruby an admonishing look that she blithely ignored. "Folks say it's my great-grandfather Eugene mainly because he's the reason his wife killed herself."

"Stories have it they had a terrible argument one night." Picking up the thread with gusto, Ruby leaned close and dropped her voice to a hush. "Seems May Storm suspected her husband of being unfaithful to her. The servants told anyone who would listen about it. Lots of bric-a-brac got broken that night." She cast a glance around the room. Mason noticed both Eli and Ruby tended to look up the stairs when they talked about the ghostly happenings.

"May had a temper when she got riled. They say that was one of the reasons her twin brother, Jeb, practically lived at the house with them." Eli sipped his coffee, distracting Mason momentarily by letting his lips linger on the edge of the mug. They looked full and flush with the heat of the liquid. Mason felt a stirring in his jeans and glanced away quickly. "He was the only one that could calm her down."

"Then others say Jeb Dahl was the reason Eugene and May fought as much as they did." Ruby gave Eli a knowing glance, and he grinned back at her.

"Her brother?" Now Mason was confused. He knew extended families lived together a lot during those years, and it wasn't unusual for in-laws to settle with a married couple for economic reasons. But May's and Jeb's family has been well-off for the times. "What was he, an ugly, no-good moocher?"

"Not at all. He was a handsome man. That was part of

the problem." Admiration shone in Ruby's voice. Mason glanced at her. "I've seen pictures of him the society pages of the old newspapers. A real cutie." She winked at him and smiled. "Like you."

Mason heard a scraping under the table, then Ruby yelped and jumped, giving Eli an evil glare. "Well, he is. And you think so too, Eli Storm. You said so."

Mason dropped his head a bit and looked at Eli over the top of his glasses, pleased at Ruby's comment -- but more pleased by the lack of denial and the bold interested look now on Eli's face. Hell, maybe the guy has a thing for screwed-up, artsy nerds!

Eli glared back at Ruby but she deflected it with a satisfied smile. "Jeb Dahl was a well-known artist in these parts, a painter. One of his paintings is in your room, Mason. That was his bedroom while he lived here."

"The seascape. I noticed. It's lovely. It's got...emotion in it." Mason smiled and admitted, "I'm an artist, too. Mostly graphics art, but I do some drawing too." He gaze lingered on Eli's handsome, bold face and strong, athletic body. "I notice gorgeous things." His cheeks burned just a bit at the double meaning he had intended to convey, but it was worth it to see the interested light in Eli's eyes heat up.

Score one for the inept flirter!

"I've got photos of Jeb I can show you." Eli pushed back from the table. "This one was taken shortly before he left town that night."

"And never came back." Ruby was getting into the

story now. "May threw herself off Mourning Cliff at dawn a week later."

Eli rose and went to a glass curio cabinet to the left of the fireplace. After removing a slender silver frame from it, he came back and handed it to Mason as he sat down. The faded sepia picture revealed a dapper young man in casual clothing of the times, light-colored hair plastered down with something heavy and glistening to keep unruly waves and long strands under control. His pale complexion and light eyes made Mason think he was a redhead. He was an attractive, slight, young man, with a handsome face lit by a contagious smile.

"She killed herself because he left town?" Mason shook his head in disbelief. "Why did he go? I thought you said he and his sister were close."

When Eli took more than a few seconds to answer Ruby took up the thread. "She killed herself because she drove him away. She was irate because she accidentally found out her brother had taken a lover. One he had been seeing for a long time."

"She killed herself over another woman?" Jeb hadn't been upset when May married his best friend, but he wasn't allowed a lover? "Wow, that's taking the close twin thing a little far."

Sitting back down at the table, Eli wrapped his hands around his coffee cup and Mason couldn't help admiring how the long fingers engulfed the wide cup and dwarfed it. Nice, strong, worn and experienced hands. Mason had to shift in his chair to give himself a little room to expand in his jeans. He wasn't erect, but this was more interest his cock had show in the mere act of watching another man in a long time. Mason had forgotten what position was the most comfortable to be in when his cock stirred to life in public. He moved his gaze up to Eli's eyes, avoiding his moist, parted lips on the way. The playful light in Eli's eyes were a little subdued.

"No, she killed herself over the fact that Jeb's lover was her husband." There was a small wry smile of reluctant acceptance of the facts on Eli's face. "May felt betrayed by the two men she loved most."

Nodding in sympathy, Ruby spared a consoling pat on the arm for Eli before turning back to Mason and the tale. "It was the talk of the town for years afterward. We all grew up with the gossip and tales about it all. There was a huge, drunken argument among the three of them that ended down in the cellars. No one knows exactly what happened, but that very night Jeb suddenly up and left. Folks said he did it to save his sister's marriage."

"Sadly, it was all for nothing." Eli sighed and refilled all of their mugs from the pot on the table. Mason clasped the warm cup with both hands, a sudden shill racing down his spine. "A week later May killed herself and left her husband with their only son to raise."

"What happened to him? I mean he lost his wife *and* his lover."

"He never remarried, never took another lover as far as anyone knows. He had a long, lonely life. He died alone during a seizure down in the cellar years later."

"That's so... sad. I can understand grieving for them, but to be alone forever... that's just...sad." Mason felt a bit of the grief for Eric he had been clinging to ease away from his heart, letting it beat a little stronger. The tight band of grief that had bound his heart had been loosening lately. He didn't want a similarly empty life spent longing for someone he'd never have again. "I don't want to be alone for the rest of my life."

"Eli's dad used to say he saw his grandfather's ghost wandering out on the cliffs in the evening, talking to Jeb like he was there with him." Ruby glanced off to the windows that faced the direction of the cliffs. "Servants said it was Jeb's picture he stared at when he was in a melancholy mood, not May's. Seems Jeb had been his sole desire, his only love, even if it had been in the closet."

"Dad just said those things to scare us kids away from playing too close to the edge." Eli scoffed and shook his head.

Mason could tell by the expression on his face he didn't believe in the ghost stories, at least not much. Eli playfully pulled at the ends of Ruby's long, graying hair. She batted away his hands but he grabbed her and hugged tight, not releasing her until she squealed in mock protest. They looked comfortable and at ease with each, like longstanding friends. Mason found himself wanting a piece of that same close camaraderie. He'd like to be in Eli's embrace, teasing or otherwise. He wanted to know more about the man.

When the two parted, Mason asked, "Are your parents still alive, Eli?"

"No. They died in the fire that took out the back section of the house. Yours?"

"No family. I'm adopted. Both my parents were in their late forties when they adopted me. I'm an only child. Neither of them had any siblings. My grandparents all died before I was ten. With Eric's death, I'm kind of... alone."

"You must be turning guys away at your door. As Ruby said," Eli smiled a smile that was full of charm, sexual interest and a touching understanding, "you're a very attractive young man, Mason."

"Thanks." He dropped his gaze for a moment and self-consciously pushed his glasses back into place. "It's been a little... rough. I-I thought Eric and I would be together until we were old and gray. It's been hard letting that idea go. I haven't felt like dating...until...until just recently. But not the guys my age who keep asking." He glanced up at Eli and straightened in the seat. "I like older guys. One's with stable lives and careers who know what they want in life. I'm kind of focused on my art, my job. I don't want to spend time with a guy whose only interest is parties, poppers, and his prick."

He glanced to his left, suddenly mindful of the third person in the room. "Sorry, Ruby."

"Don't worry. I've heard worse, Mason. Said worse!" She patted his arm again. "Hell, every time I'm here and I smell brandy in the air when I know darn well there isn't any thing but wine in the whole place, I get a chill and I *think* much worse than that." She sniffed the air and subtly looked around at the growing shadows in the subtly lit, furniture-filled room. "It always makes me wonder if May isn't haunting the place. Folks say she took to drink quite a bit before she died. Was probably drunk when she jumped. I'd have to be."

Unable to stop himself, Mason glanced around and hunched deeper into the couch and lap quilt. The flickering glow from the hearth made the shadows dance with long legs over the walls. A chill slid down his back as Mason remembered the face in the bathroom mirror and blurted out, "The ghost's a man."

"What? How would you know that, Mason?" Eli's voice sounded normal, like he was asking how he knew Eli's favorite color -- which was green if the color of the great cashmere and wool sweaters the man wore everyday was anything to go by. Mason defended the personal observation by reassuring himself artists were supposed to notice things like color and texture, especially if it brought the green flecks in dark brown, hungry eyes.

"In the mirror...upstairs. I thought I saw a face in the steam. It wouldn't rub off the glass, not even with a towel, but when I turned around and then back, it was completely gone like it had never been there. I know it sounds crazy, but...it was a man's face."

"Are you sure?" Where there was disbelief in Eli's face, Ruby's was full of eager interest. "Is it Eugene Storm? I bet it is. I've been trying to make contact with him for years but he never wants to talk to me." Ruby's eyes darted back and forth while she scrutinized every pore on Mason's face. "*You* he would like, Mason. You look a lot like Jeb. I can see him choosing you to contact."

"Ruby, stop it." Eli was firm, even a little harsh. "Mason came here to rest and sort things out. He's still getting over a big loss." He ran a sympathetic gaze over Mason.

"Don't fill his artistic head with dead lovers' ghosts and suicide." He looked away, a little reluctant when he added, "He doesn't need any help imagining things here."

Eli's lack of support hurt him more than Mason thought it could. They had known each other only a few days, but Mason was comfortable in the man's presence; he even felt a certain security being with Eli. But, now, it was painfully obvious that Eli thought of him as some fragile, potentially suicidal dork.

For the first time in ages, Mason had the energy to let his temper flare. He tossed aside the quilt and stood up.

"I'm not imagining it. The face was there." He started to tell them about the hand touching him in the middle of the night and out at the cliff, but stopped himself. He could tell Eli didn't believe him as it was. "Excuse me. I'm going to read in my room. Mind if I borrow one of these?" He pulled an old, clothbound book off one of the library shelves and hefted it, not even looking at the title.

Eli stood up but didn't approach him. He shrugged his shoulders, a look of regret on his face. "Sure. Go ahead. They all belonged to my grandfather and his father. I've never had time or inclination to do more that glance at them. I don't even know what's up there, but help yourself."

Grudgingly, Mason nodded his head, clutching the book hard to help stem his feelings. "Thanks. Don't hold supper for me, okay? I'm not hungry."

Humiliated and hurt, Mason strode to the staircase and fled to his ghost-infested room, the last place he really wanted to be.

§ § §

He'd read for a short time but the book he'd randomly grabbed, *The Perennial Bachelor*, a 1925 edition by Anne Parrish, told the tale of a wealthy bachelor and the decadence of the elite society that he represented. The story was unedited and the characters lacked depth. Mason quickly lost interest. But the artist in him admired the book's beautiful binding, and he leafed through the unread pages. He stopped short at the inside front cover. In the same instant, he felt the prickle of the blood draining from his face. The marbled paper bore an inscription, written in fading peacock-green ink, in the flowing script of the day: *To Jeb, who means the most. Most fondly, Eugene.* Mason stared dumbly at the page for a moment, then set the book aside with a silent vow to check the other books on the shelves downstairs for similar dedications. The discovery had brought a shiver and slight quake to Mason's hands and body, and the warm comforter on the bed beckoned.

Depressed over the conversation with Eli, chilled by the note from a dead man's hand, Mason turned in early. His alarm clock barely rolled over to show 7:00 p.m. on its glowing, red face when he stripped, pulled on a pair of flannel sleep pants, and fell into bed. He was asleep within minutes of crawling under the covers.

For the first time since sleeping in this bedroom he had closed the window all the way making sure no misty breezes could disturb his sleep or fuel is imagination.

He halfway believed in ghosts before coming here. Or maybe it was just his loneliness that make him start in the middle of the night thinking he had felt the mattress dip as Eric rolled into bed long weeks after Eric was alive to do that. The sensation had faded overtime, but this inn was bringing it all back. And it wasn't Eric visiting him. That face in the mirror hadn't looked anything like Eric or felt like Eric. It was definitely a stranger to Mason, if not to this room. He bet Eugene Storm had been here many a night if he and Jeb had been secret lovers.

Burying his head in a pillow and pulling the cover up over his shoulders for good measure, Mason blocked out the faint beams of moonlight that filter through the curtains and the sounds of the choruses of peepers.

The warm, engulfing comfort of the quilts and soft mattress appealed to him on a number of levels, but mostly for the opportunity to be wrapped in the snug embrace of flannel and down and let his worries drift away on the soothing void of sleep. Since he didn't have a warm, loving body beside him anymore and none in the foreseeable future, he'd learned to find substitutes for comfort. A warm fire and Eli's company had been doing a fine job of it until the last few moments. He couldn't that Eli thought he was suicidal. What he couldn't believe even more was that he'd been crazy enough to blurt out he'd seen a ghost. Looking back at it he really couldn't blame Eli but the man's response had still stung.

Every reason he hated dating came rushing back to him and along with it came a bitter ached over the loss of Eric, his own self-appointed short comings and a loneliness that he desperately wanted to have banished, at least for a little while.

His dreams came like wisps of smoke, elusive and faint. They slowly increased and wrapped around him like tendrils from a campfire, reaching out to smother him with the scent of brandy-dowsed flames and scorching caresses to his chilled skin. The strands of smoke turned into flesh and blood arms and the heat on his body became hard palms and even harder thighs.

A heavy weight pressed Mason into the mattress and he sighed at the sensation, having gone too long with the pleasure of another's solidness against his chest, his belly, parting his thighs and nestling between them. His cock stirred and swelled as hands explored his shoulders and arms, ran down his sides, pressed against his ribs, tousled his hair, and caressed his cheek. They seemed to be everywhere at once, tweaking nipples to taut ripeness, soothing parted lips as he gasped in unexpected pleasure, and kneading the firm muscles of his clenched ass.

The hands and arms turned connected to a strong, long body and Mason could see and feel a trail of dark hair over the broad chest that trailed down to disappear between their grinding bellies and hips. He followed the trail back up and this time the face was clear, frame din dark curly hair with gentle brown eyes and a half-amused smile that Eli had worn since the first time Mason had looked up into his face. Eli had been embracing him then, too, but Mason much preferred this kind of hold to tone Eli had used to stop him from falling into the fire.

His pleasure built with each grinding roll of Eli's hips. Mason and silently willed his orgasm to hold back a few seconds longer. Then a chill settled over him and the solid, secure weight on top of his body dissolved away to be replaced with a smoky cloud of cold dread. His climax waned and Mason started awake.

Flat on his back, instantly awake, and eyes wide open, he looked up into a enveloping shroud of white mist. A blurred image of the face from the mirror hovered over his own close enough that if it had breathed, Mason would have felt the air moving on his skin. He didn't need his glasses to see this.

"Jesus!"

Bolting upright, Mason waved his arms to dispel the mist, the cloying smell of brandy clinging to his nostrils, the mist making his eyes water. He flung the covers to one side and jumped out of the bed.

As he stood half-naked and barefoot shaking, trembling with the cold that had seeped into the room and the rush of adrenaline racing through his veins, Mason watched the blurred face in the mist linger over the empty spot where he had been lying then slowly drift toward the window and ease out through the cracks between the panes.

The window was still firmly shut, but the curtains fluttered as if catch in a gentle a breeze. Once the mist had left the room, Mason decided the ghost had the right idea. He rocketed out the bedroom door and down the hallway, slowing only long enough to navigate the stairs without his glasses.

§ § §

"I don't care if you don't believe me. There's a ghost

in this house. In my room. I'm not sleeping there alone." Mason barely waited until the bedroom door was open before he barged past its sleepy-eyed occupant and strode to the obviously unused side of the just recently vacated queen-sized bed. "I'm not sleeping *anywhere* alone in this inn. So make room. I'm freezing."

Shivering, he grabbed a handful of blankets, sheets and comforters and pulled them back far enough that he could slip under them without disturbing the used half of the bed.

"*What?*" Still standing with the handle of the open door in his hand and a bewildered look on his face, Eli swiveled his head around to watch Mason storm across the room.

It was obvious Eli was going to need more time to process what had just happened than Mason planned on giving to him. Mason ignored the man and his confusion. He punched a pillow into a shape with blows that promised to have the room raining feathers if the pillow didn't submit to his demands soon. Luckily for all, it went meekly. Satisfied, Mason jammed it against the headboard and threw his head down on it, back turned to the door and to Eli.

He couldn't trust himself to look at the man whose bed he had just climbed into uninvited. He had thought about being in Eli's bed -- just not under these circumstances.

He was still shaking. That ghostly face had almost kissed him, he knew it. He was scared out of his wits and he didn't care who knew it. This wasn't going to change anything. Eli couldn't possibly think less of him after this afternoon.

"Don't hog the blankets." He kicked his feet further under the covers and pulled the folded-back edge up under his chin. "And please tell me you don't snore." He looked up and over his shoulder to throw Eli an accusing glare, then closed his eyes tightly and buried the side of his face in the cushion again. "But it doesn't really *matter.*" He squeezed the words out through tightly clenched teeth. "I'm not leaving." He pulled the covers around himself until they hugged him as snuggly as plastic food wrap.

Eli shut the door and walked to the newly occupied side of his bed. Mason tracked his progress by sound, refusing to look up even when he felt Eli sit on the edge of the bed beside him.

"Mason?"

It was the warm, strong hand that rubbed comfortingly over his shoulder that finally prompted Mason to turn his head to one side. He pried open one eye so he could peer up into Eli's face. Eli's expression was part concern, part affectionate amusement, and part something else. It was the *something else* that kept Mason from being angry about the amused portion. Embarrassment still tried to muster a glow to his cheeks but being scared witless won out. He felt cold. His chest ached from his lungs' attempt to keep up with the pounding heart that had lodged at the base of his throat.

Christ, he couldn't believe that…that…*thing…* had touched him, hovered over him eye to eye and…whatever other body parts that had lined up. He'd have much preferred waking up to the man in his dream doing all that — the mostly-naked, clothed only in a pair of loose boxers, sexy man currently trying to hold back laughter while leaning in close and rubbing Mason's shoulder with a deliciously hot hand.

"Want to sit up here and tell me what happened?"

Mason looked up, trying to pack as much determination into his expression as a one-eyed glare could give. "I don't care if you think I'm a clueless, suicidal dork nerd." He pulled the cover more tightly around his shoulder, shrugging off Eli's warm and pleasant but, nevertheless, placating touch. "I'm not leaving this bed until morning." He suddenly sat up to reach over and turn back the rumpled covers on the other side of the bed invitingly. "And neither are you." He scooted his bare-chested body back down under the blankets, his haste nearly dislodging Eli from his seat on the mattress edge. "Because, *I repeat*, I am *not* sleeping alone."

Silence filled the room broken, only by the sound of Mason, face back in the pillow, gasping and gulping air, trying to breathe through the sack of feathers.

"Okay. Let's try this another way." Eli walked around to his side of the bed and crawled in. He turned on his side to face Mason and pulled the covers up to his waist. Mason hoped he had settled in for the night. But, when the lamp on the side table remained lit, Mason steeled himself for more questions.

"Tell me what happened in your room, Mason. You really believe in hauntings?"

"Ghosts!" It was a barely understandable yelp muffled by the pillow.

"Spirits, ghost, poltergeists." Eli's voice was gentle but firm. "They don't exist."

Mason rolled over onto his back then curled onto his side facing Eli. "You haven't had one touch you in the middle of the night, or look at you in the bathroom mirror or run an icy cold hand up your back and sit beside you at the cliffs." His voice rose with each sentence, shaky and hoarse.

He forced himself to stop and take a deep breath, hoping a calmer effort would make the disbelief fade a bit from Eli's handsome face. It only lasted a moment before the memory of what had happened in the room flooded him with a hollow, terrified flush again. He felt as if he might throw up.

"You didn't just wake up with one lying on top of you." He could feel the heat radiating off Eli's skin -- warm, human, alive.

"He...*it*...was going to..." — Mason took a deep, shaky breath but the words came out soft and small anyway, full of fear and disgust — "...kiss me." He had to fight back the tears, but he knew his face had twisted into a deep frown. The fear that had sung through every fiber of his being only moments before lingered. He was helpless as his whole body shook.

Eli sighed, pushing back the covers and revealing his own torso and Mason's.

Mason was sure that the exasperated man was preparing to throw him out of the bed. He gripped the sheet tighter.

"Come here, baby." The words were low and deep, the sound rich, soothing and so gentle with compassionate understanding that Mason couldn't bear it. He made to roll out of the bed, but he didn't get far.

Eli yanked Mason toward him in a won't-take-no-for-an-answer bear hug. Mason's eyes popped wide. His heart, which might have been slowing just a fraction, began to race in earnest – 'though for a much more pleasant reason than before. They were naked chest to naked chest, and nose to nose, groins so close that body parts jostled and rubbed. Even slightly blurry in a soft out-of-focus way, Eli was amazingly handsome. He smelled good, too -- woodsy and clean. Mason broke out in a cold sweat.

"I've got you."

That was all it took. Three words and Mason's last vestige of control snapped and the tears poured down his cheeks. They were mixed with gasps, sniffles, and broken sentences. "I mean...I haven't kissed any one in almost, shit!-almost *two* years. Nobody!" A surge of righteous anger pushed terror aside. "If any lips are going to be pressing on mine from now on, they sure as *hell* aren't going to be cold, d-dead ones!"

He stuttered and gasped, half the time burying his head under Eli's chin wiping away his slowing tears on the man's hot skin, and the other half staring wildly up into Eli's silent, watchful face. "I mean, if someone's lips are going to kiss me, I want them to be warm and firm and wet and ..." -- Mason swallowed hard, his gaze darting back and forth between Eli's eyes to read his expression and his lips to stare at their full, wet goodness -- "attached to a living, b-breathing man."

Mason became aware of Eli's hand running soothing strokes over his shoulders and down his back, slipping easily under the waistband of his loose flannel sleep pants and lingering on the curve at the small of his back. It was exciting and distracting.

"A man with strong hands, not one made out of mist." His voice faltered and the fluttering in his gut changed from fear to desire. He'd had a hard-on threatening to burst to life the moment he'd fled his own room. Now his cock was fully engorged, heavy, hot and eager. It poked Eli's abdomen, but the man didn't pull back from the embrace in which he had Mason wrapped.

Mason managed to hold his gaze still long enough to look Eli in the eye. His own hands began exploring the warm flesh he was pressed against, growing bolder when he didn't meet any resistance. "One with dark hair and dark, kind, compassionate eyes and a name that's easy to whisper. *Eli?*"

"Like I said, baby, I've got you."

Eli's dark-eyed stare caressed Mason's face and his hungry soul. Mason's breathing came in jerky, little gulps. He couldn't stop his limbs from trembling. He was a mess and he knew it. But, Eli's powerful embrace calmed Mason's quaking nerves, giving him a sense of security and protection he hadn't felt in a very long time.

And, none of that seemed to matter the moment Eli's lips touched his.

They were hot and firm, commanding and gentle. Just what Mason needed right at that moment, a calm, in-charge kiss while locked in a tight embrace. The controlled passion Mason saw in Eli's eyes made him feel safe, warm, cared for. It let him know he was desired, but that this wasn't going to go any farther than Mason wanted it to. It could be a comfort kiss to sooth and reassure, or it could be the start of a passionate night filled with exploration and discovery. He knew the choice was his.

He just didn't know which way to run, forward or backward. Mason's brain spun in circles. Backward held ghosts -- several different kinds of them -- and loneliness. Lots and lots of loneliness. Forward lay a future that was blurry at best, but it at least held a chance at happiness. The future held a chance to chase away his demons. All of them -- the one from upstairs and the one he'd brought with him.

A hand slipped under the loose elastic waistband of his pants and kneaded his ass while a gently exploring tongue parted his lips and pressed against his teeth until they opened. Wet warmth invaded his mouth and Mason groaned as his cock shot up in what seemed like a ridiculous attempt to touch Eli's tongue tip to tip. Blood rushed to the surface of his flesh and a tingling glow bathed his skin. God, this felt good. So. Damned. Good.

Thinking went out the window and Mason ran full tilt toward forward. He slid his hands up Eli's neck to cup the man's head and pulled him closer, devouring Eli's mouth with a long pent-up hunger that made both of them moan.

Things turned fast and furious. They stripped off their sleep pants under the covers. They weren't entirely successful at discarding them, though. Kicking the pants aside still left them twisted in the jumble of sheets. Mason didn't know where to put his hands first so he put them everywhere – on defined, hard muscles and on thick, firm thighs. He threaded his fingers through dark waves of hair, slid his palms over satiny smooth hips and traced the thick tufts of chest hair down to the wiry bush of pubic hair at the base of Eli's stout, eager cock. Then he did it all over again, his own hips thrusting in rhythm to the grip Eli's strong hand had on both their cocks. Mason's brain was divided between the delicious sensations the hand was pulling from his hypersensitive prick to the metal-melting heat of the searing kiss Eli's lips and tongue were blistering his mouth with. The kiss threatened to suck all the air from his lungs and his ability to reason from his brain. Far too quickly for both Mason's ego and his enjoyment, his orgasm boiled up from the pit of his abdomen, grabbed his balls and shot out his prick.

Mason cried out and froze, body stiff with surprise and the sudden spasm of a climax so strong and so unexpected his eyes watered. He buried his face in the crook of Eli's neck, his soft cries muffled by muscled shoulder as a litany of gentle encouragement and comfort whispered in his ear. A powerful arm held him tightly to Eli's chest like a hot band of steel, anchoring and reassuring.

Mason opened his eyes and tilted his head to one side. Nope, no mist, no half-formed, white faces, and -- even if he was blurry -- it was definitely Eli. This wasn't a dream or a solo effort in the shower. He was in the arms of a lover, a warm, tender, attentive new lover. A lover who still had an impressive erection.

The scene clicked into focus again as his climax faded and his hearing finally distinguished the words his mind had just accepted.

"It's okay, baby. I've got you. I've got you."

God, he hoped Eli meant that for more than just now. Now that he'd jumped back into the dating pool, he didn't plan to leave the water any time soon. The hollow ache that had taken up most of the space in his chest lately crumpled like used newspaper, receding to a place deeper inside of him. It was still there, but smaller and less painful. He could breathe a little easier and he felt like his heart had more space in his chest. It was odd, but vaguely exciting, as if he'd been offered a new adventure.

Eli kept up stroking both cocks, slowing his rhythm as Mason relaxed, the caress now wet and smooth with the addition of Mason's cum. Mason's embarrassment at shooting off so quickly faded as his cock stirred and grew with each sensual flick of Eli's large, experienced hand and wrist.

Looking up into Eli's face, a rush of uncertainty washed through Mason until Eli smiled. "I got you, Mace. And in case you're worried, I'm not letting go."

Mason pulled back a few more inches to get the other man's features into marginally sharper focus. At least Mason could judge what his partner was thinking more easily when he could read his expression. The smile was genuine and the hungry look in Eli's face seemed tempered with a sparkle of tenderness.

Christ, the man was gorgeous in ordinary daylight. But, flushed, sweaty and crushing Mason to his naked, aroused body, Eli Storm was an overwhelming god of sensual power. Mason wanted him so bad, he could taste it -- or he wanted to.

"Please, tell me you have condoms?" Was that actually his voice begging? God, he was desperate.

"Uh-uh. We'll have to do it the safe way this time. We'll have to save more adventurous ways to enjoy each other for next time." Eli dropped a lingering kiss on Mason's lips then nuzzled around Mason's jaw line and down his neck. "After I hit the drug store."

"Shit!"

Eli's strokes sped up, and Mason's hips began to buck in time to them. It was great, but not enough. He wanted more contact, more closeness than another hand job, even a great one. He ground his body to Eli's and wrapped his arms around his lover's broad shoulders, hands clenched into fists pressed hard against Eli's back.

In silent understanding of what Mason needed, Eli abruptly stopped and peeled Mason from his leech-like hold.

Mason was suddenly seized by doubt. "What's wrong?"

Wordlessly, Eli rolled Mason away from him. Then, he swiftly dragged him back so they were spooning, Eli's chest to Mason's back. He urged Mason to lift his leg and, when he did, Eli slid his thick, cum-coated cock along Mason's sensitive perineum. He clamped Mason's leg back down, and began thrusting so that his shaft slid in and out of the tight embrace of Mason's legs and ass cheeks, his cock's tip nudging Mason's balls on each forward stroke.

Eli used one arm to plaster Mason tightly to him while his other traveled over Mason's chest to pinch and rub both tiny nubs of rosy flesh. He drew a lazy path down the smaller man's smooth skin to take hold of Mason's neglected cock. "Like this?" Eli breathed into Mason's the damp strands of Mason's hair, and the heat of his breath scalded Mason's scalp where it touched.

At a loss for words, panting for breath, Mason could only nod and then groan as Eli picked up the pace and sensation assaulted him. This time the building tension rose faster, 'though it was more defined.

The heat of Eli's body, the power of his hold, the tone of his murmured pleasure and gasping need tossed fuel on the fire raging in Mason's veins. Mason was engulfed in flame, and each stroke from Eli's hand and cock stoked the blaze higher. Harsh, needy kisses marked his neck and Mason turned his head to meet the lips with his own, eagerly accepting Eli's demanding, ravenous kiss.

His mind reeled and fireworks exploded behind his closed eyes. His own climax pumped from his cock with Eli's willing fingers at the same time that he felt a sudden liquid heat bath his ass and inner thighs. The wet, sexy sound of moist flesh on moist flesh joined the scent of freshly spilled semen and forced Mason's already powerful, already exquisite climax higher. He went rigid as he came, body plastered to Eli's, legs pressed closely around Eli's cock, stoking the pleasure of Eli's orgasm.

The powerful shuddering of Eli's body drove the words from him. "God, Mace, what you do to me. Jesus!"

The deep, satisfied groan in his ear was like a reward, and Mason grinned with pride, thrilled that he had satisfied Eli by simply being wrapped around him. It spoke well for future, more adventurous activities.

"If this is what being scared does to you, I'm buying an entire library of horror movies." Eli squeezed and Mason yelped.

"Bastard, let go." He pushed and prodded until he had turned in Eli's arms enough to lie on his side and face the other man. It please Mason that Eli's hold only loosened instead of letting go.

And, even he could see the broad smile on Eli's face. The affection and lust still in Eli's dark eyes were enough for Mason to forgive the man's skepticism – 'though Eli's gentle chuckle threatened the forgiveness.

"It's not funny. There *was* a ghost in my bed." Mason narrowed his eyes and flattened his lips into what he knew was a thin, unhappy line. "And not the one you're thinking of. I didn't bring this one with me. It's *your* ghost, not mine!"

"Mason, Eugene Storm is dead."

"Which would be at least a basic requirement to be a ghost, don't you think?"

Eli had to concede that point, and he did with a small shrug.

Mason ventured more. "Maybe...maybe he has unfinished business here."

"Like what?"

Eli was trying to be understanding, but Mason could hear it in Eli's voice. He was humoring Eli.

"Like maybe he's looking for his lover? He's been

haunting Jeb's bedroom, dogging my tracks because I'm sleeping in there. Maybe we just need to tell him Jeb is gone?"

Suddenly he felt a pang of sympathy for Eugene Storm. He knew how lost he'd felt when Eric was suddenly gone from his life. Jeb had disappeared from Storm's life just as unexpectedly.

"If they're both dead, and they *are*, don't you think he'd know that already?"

"How do I know what dead people know? Is that what mediums do? Talk to the dead?"

"I don't know any professional mediums."

Mason's frowned. He had to beat back a sudden burn of tears. This was frustrating, seeing the ghost and having no one believe it existed.

"How about a séance or something? Got a Ouija board?"

Eli snorted lightly, softening it with a gentle smile and quick kiss to Mason's furrowed brow. "Well, Ruby's done a couple of Halloween party séances, but --"

"Let's ask her! Ruby believes in the ghost!" A thrill raced through Mason at the prospect of a real séance to reach an actual ghost. He loved scary movies, but now he'd been thrust into one of his own. It was more intimidating and terrifying, but at least in a séance he wouldn't be alone if the ghost showed up.

"Mason--"

"Please, Eli? For me? For my peace of mind?" He

hated pleading, but he honestly didn't think he could take another wake-up call like his last one. "I can't sleep in that bedroom another night until this is cleared up. It's too creepy."

"I wasn't planning on letting you sleep there." Eli leaned in close and pinned Mason to the mattress. He silenced Mason's token protest with a heated kiss and a rib-bruising embrace.

Mason pushed Eli back when the man came in for a second taste. "So you're going to get Ruby to have a séance and get rid of old Eugene once and for all?"

Eli hung his head in defeat. "Okay." He chuckled, a whatever-it-takes-to-keep-you-happy look on his face. Then the accommodating expression turned mischievous, and he nipped at Mason's neck. "If the spirit moves me."

"Not funny." Mason had to mumble between brief but insistent kisses.

Eli hugged Mason to his chest and chuckled into his wayward tufts of fine, dark hair. "To you, maybe."

§ § §

"Are you sure we shouldn't turn on another light?"

Mason glanced around the gloom-shrouded room, dubiously eyeing the closed wooden sliding doors that cut them off from the rest of the big, old, creaky house. "Maybe that one in the corner?"

"It has to be shadowy, Mason, or the spirits won't feel comfortable coming to us." Ruby patted the cushioned chair beside her, then motioned to Mason to move closer. He hesitated, but approached her. "Now relax." She patted the chair again as if she had to subdue it for Mason to sit on it. "Sit down here beside me. On my right."

Mason cautiously slid into place where she wanted him. He darted an anxious glance toward Eli, who was sitting on Ruby's other side. He looked over his shoulder at the advancing shadows as the evening sun disappeared, taking with it even the faint glow behind the curtains. He searched his memory of every horror movie that he'd ever seen, and couldn't recall a single séance that had taken place in broad daylight.

They were seated in the small library, once an old parlor room. Oak bookcases lined the walls, full to brimming with rows and stacks of books and odd items. The floor was thick with the same sort of oriental rugs that Mason has seen in the lobby. The carpet muffled sound eerily. Two loveseats and a stool filled supplied the remaining furniture. Thin threads of incense smoke drifted up from ashtrays, and Mason recognized the scent of sandalwood and cinnamon.

Sliding his chair to the right along the table, Mason edged closer to Eli's reassuringly large presence. The antique, oval library table had occupied a corner until Mason and Eli had hefted its mass to the center of the room. The table was small enough that all three people could touch hands.

In the middle of the small sheet-draped table sat three, white, unlit candles and Ruby's black and brown Ouija board. It looked out-of-date and well used, and Mason surmised that Ruby had gotten the board as a child.

"Let me have the book, please."

Ruby held out her hand expectantly and Mason thrust into it Jeb's gift from Eugene, the book that he had been reading the night before.

"What's this for again?"

"The book obviously belonged to both men at one point, a gift from Eugene to Jeb from the inscription you mentioned. I'm going to use it to focus on, to see if I can reach Eugene Storm through it."

Mason couldn't help giving her a skeptical look. Eli just smiled at him and then turned his attention to playing with the little plastic planchette sitting on the Ouija board.

Slightly defensive, Ruby huffed and moved closer to the table. "They say it really helps to have a personal belonging from the departed spirit to draw it back. Kind of like a psychic who has to touch items to get a vision." She checked the inscription in the front of the book and then placed it in front of her. Looking up, she glared across the table, snatched the planchette from Eli's fiddling fingers and centered it over the middle of the playing board.

The alphabet ranged over most of the Ouija board, arched in two rows. Under those ran a straight line of numbers from one to zero. On the top left corner sat the word *yes* and on the right, *no*. An ominous *farewell* occupied the bottom line. In the middle of the small planchette was a hole large enough to reveal one letter or number on the board. The little wedge was designed to slip across the board on three tiny, padded feet. Mason didn't know about anyone else, but he thought the chain of bones running around the outside of the board subtracted just-for-fun elements from the game. He cast another glance over his shoulder, looking longingly at the closed doors that marked the room's only easy exit.

"We ready?"

When he didn't respond, Ruby squeezed Mason's hand to regain his attention. Startled, he flinched and jerked his head back around.

"You sure you want to do this, Mace?" Eli held the hand that Ruby didn't. He squeezed it reassuringly. "We don't have to, you know."

The heat from Eli's skin was warm comfort, anchoring Mason to the living. His own fingers felt numb and cold, and his heart thumped faster than usual in his chest. Mason wet his dry lips, settled a wide-eyed, contact-enhanced stare on his new lover and nodded. He blew out a breath to steady his nerves.

"I'm good. Let's do this."

Mason reluctantly extracted his hands from this partners' grasp and put his fingers hand on the planchette. Ruby lifted them off gently. "First we call the spirit to us. Then we see if he'll talk to us."

Frowning, Mason dropped his hands on table and glanced around the room again.

Ruby settled herself more comfortably in her seat and looked from Eli to Mason and back again. "Let's all take a deep breath and relax. Try to clear your thoughts and open your minds." She took a deep, noisy breath, held it, then slowly exhaled, nodding at both men to follow her example.

Eli wore an expression of amused cooperation, but he neither rolled his eyes nor did he sigh in exasperation as Mason expected him to. When he caught Mason staring at him, watching his shirt pull tight across his broad chest as it expanded with each deep breath, Eli gave Mason a sultry little smile and a seductive wink that brought a flush of heat to Mason's neck and face.

Mason's gaze rested on Eli's strong, confident face. His fear retreated for a moment, crowded out by Eli's beauty and Mason's memories of their time together in bed. Eli was thoughtful., experienced, patient. Mason could still feel Eli's muscles rippling against his body, his strong hands roving over Mason, his beautiful eyes crinkled by the laugh that both soothed and unnerved Mason. A little of the tension eased from Mason's shoulders and his next deep breath felt less constricted – even if his jeans were suddenly tighter and he had to shift his legs to make room for his growing erection. He dropped his gaze, but it landed on Eli's folded hands. Mason's thoughts wandered just a bit, as he noticed not for the first time that Eli had nice hands, strong, tanned, experienced hands just the way Mason liked them. Eli was his anchor in that moment and would be his anchor through the séance – far past the séance, too.

Ruby rapped on the table to get their attention. "Focus, guys." Eli flashed Mason a passionate glance and Ruby tersely added, "On the ghost, not on each other."

Closing his eyes to resist temptation, Mason took several deep breaths and tried to clear his mind as Ruby had instructed. But the face in the mirror, the same face that had hovered over him in bed, kept forming in his mind. It unnerved him and at the same time offered a strange hope, a hope that perhaps the ghost was near and would become visible to both Eli and Ruby.

Mason raised a hand to push nervously at the bridge of his glasses before he remembered he was wearing his contacts -- but only because he'd asked Eli to get them from his room. He'd flatly refused to go back there for any reason.

With a sigh, he turned his attention back to the board. He needed to concentrate but since his had libido reawakened, it was harder and harder to think of anything but Eli.

"Can you get the light, Eli? I'm going to light the candles." Eli moved away and Mason's eyes followed him to the lamp. A touch of panic hit him when the room went dark save for the sputtering flame from three tiny wicks. Shadows leapt out at him, then huddled close like a blanket of blackest velvet.

"We do this by just candle light?" Mason's panic receded slightly when Eli regained the seat next to him.

"Of course. The candles channel the energy in the room, to guide a spirit to our midst." Speaking calmly in a hushed version of her normally cheerful voice, Ruby had lit all three candles and placed one about a foot in front of each of them. "Give them a moment to focus their power."

The flickering light cast ghastly, pale shadows on their surroundings and made the contours of their facial features appear hollow and gaunt. All the sounds in the small room seemed magnified and hushed at the same time to Mason. The tick of the clock on the mantle dominated the room, but the usually crisp click was muted as if a pillow had been placed over it. The crickets and the peepers had begun their song outside in moonlight-drenched dark, but the singsong tune was muffled behind the thick velvet drapes. The walls seemed closer than they'd been when the three of them had sat down only a minute ago.

Mason's pulse began to accelerated as Ruby continued her preparations, and a cold hand touched his neck. "I don't think we need the candles, Ruby."

"Concentrate on breathing deep and emptying your mind." Ruby had closed her eyes. Her hands were spread across Jeb's book and her face was smooth and relaxed, voice more hushed, almost a whisper. "I'm trying to reach out to the spirit world."

"I don't think we need to anymore." Mason knew his voice had a tremor in it, but he couldn't help it. The room had turned cooler, darker, quieter. Even the peepers outside had stopped their song. Mason shivered.

"Are you all right, Mace?" Eli opened his eyes when Mason's voice cracked. He instantly reached across the small table and gripped Mason's forearm.

"Not really. I think the spirit world is reaching out to us. He's here." Mason pointed at the Ouija board with a trembling finger.

"Christ!" Eli's grip was going to leave behind bruises, but Mason didn't mind. It was reassuring and it kept him from running out of the room like a scared little boy.

"Oh, my God! Eugene Storm! It's true." Ruby gasped. Her fingers had wrapped tightly around the edge of the book until her knuckles paled, but now she shoved it further out into the table's center, away from her, as if it had been on fire.

Hovering over the dime-store Ouija board was a white wisp. The strand of mist churned in the air, growing larger and denser as they watched. While Mason, Eli and Ruby withdrew their hands in astonishment and horror, the little planchette quivered and then slowly glided from one letter to the next, spending only a few seconds on each. The felt pads whispered on the board as the planchette traveled, but the sound seemed like a ghostly wail to Mason.

"Oh, God. I hope someone has a better memory than I do!" Ruby squinted to read the letters as the little saucer slid to the other end of the board. "M-O…"

Eli called out the letter closest to his end of the table. "V-E-M-Y-B…"

"O-N-E-S." Mason found his voice, calling out the letter in a harsh whisper.

"M-O-V-E-M-Y-B-O-N-E-S." He frowned and tried to make words from it. "Movem by ones? No, wait. That's wrong."

"Movemy b ones?"

"Uh-uh, guys. Try *move my bones.*"

The saucer rested on the S, unmoving and silent. The mist tumbled and swirled over the board, gathering form as it became denser. While Mason stared into its depths, the outline of a human face with rough, unfinished features slowly formed before him. Even though he could see the face, Mason could also see through it, like a misty overlay on a photo layout. The ghost shifted and suddenly it lay perfectly over Eli's handsome frown. Mason swallowed hard and fervently hoped the visual wouldn't haunt him. Then the candles flickered and extinguished themselves, pitching the room into total darkness.

"Sit still. I'll get the lights."

Mason felt and heard a bump, then a scratch cast a tiny circle of gold light in the darkness when a match flared. Ruby had re-lit the three candles by the time Eli found his way to the lamp. Now the room was ablaze with soft electric sunlight that pulled the shadows from their corners and tossed them out into the night.

Crouching down beside Mason's chair, Eli ran both hands up Mason's arms, rubbing and warming the limbs as they shivered and quaked under his touch. "That's what chased you out of your room?"

All Mason could manage was a jerky nod. He tried twice to speak before he was able to sputter the words. "MOVE MY BONES! He's not in a *cemetery*?" Mason stared accusingly at Eli but didn't pull away from his comforting touch. "He isn't in the basement or anything, is he?"

"Of course not." Eli scoffed. "Eugene Storm was buried in the graveyard in town. I remember going to his funeral as a kid."

"Guys," Ruby's voice was full of amazement and the smug excitement of discovery. The men turned to look at her. She was staring at the last pages in the book Mason had given her. "I don't think it's Eugene we were talking to."

"What?" Mason had been completely convinced that it was Eugene who was haunting his room. It didn't make sense that it might be anyone but Eugene.

"Who else could it be?" Eli's question seemed to confirm that he'd come around to believing Mason whole-heartedly.

"Look at this." Holding the book up, Ruby flipped a few pages back and forth, showing them several paragraphs of a handwritten entry. "It's written on the blank pages in the back of this book." Mason and Eli took in the handwritten lines. Ruby read a few lines to herself.

"Jeb Dahl," she whispered.

"What?" Eli still hadn't let go of Mason, and still crouched beside him. Mason's teeth chattered lightly when he tried to take a deep breath.

"Listen to this." She ran a finger down the page, squinting in the dim light.

"It's with a heavy heart I write this, but I can no longer bear the burden of this horrible knowledge alone.

Decades ago, I cast the ashes of my wife off Mourning Cliff. It seemed fitting she should be free to travel the ocean and the winds to find the happiness I couldn't give her in life. It was one less weight that my soul had to carry.

But the greater burden remains, even after all these years, like a festering wound, consuming me from within. I only hope confessing the crimes for which I am responsible will allow my family to understand that they were done in the name of love: Love for my faithful and loving wife May and love for her dear brother Jeb. I hope my words help their spirits rest in peace. May is gone and my beloved Jeb is dead these many years as well.

Dead and gone from life by his own sister's hand.

On the fifteenth of October, 1925, May to discovered Jeb and me in a passionate, unquestionably compromising state in the wine cellar. Enraged and possibly temporarily unbalanced by the shock, May took up an iron pinning rod from a wine rack and struck her brother down. The blow to Jeb's head was instantly fatal. I escaped her ire only because the magnitude of her actions registered instantly on her, in the way that Jeb crumpled to the floor and in the blood-splattered walls. The only color on her face and hands was Jeb's own blood, and for the next week she never stopped washing them. A week to the hour after she killed the brother than she so loved, May leapt from Mourning Cliff. Unable to wash the bloodstains from the cellar walls, and unable to bear standing there a moment longer, I sealed the room to prevent discovery of May's shame and mine.

Under cover of night, I buried my beloved Jeb at the top of Mourning Cliff, his grave marked by the white shore stone and my well-worn footsteps on the dirt. I go to him regularly and we pass the time together in spirit.

May never recovered from that night, and it is a sad lament to say she is undoubtedly happier on the winds and sea then she was as my wife. As for Jeb, my heart has always been with him. He was my sole desire in life, and in death he will be my soul's only desire for all time.

Eugene Storm

October 15, 1964

"Jeb Dahl. The ghost must be Jeb, not Eugene. All of them. They all died for love, even Eugene. Oh, my, Eli. I'm so sorry." Reaching out, Ruby laid a comforting hand on Eli's arm.

Eli stood and, distracted, ran a hand over his face. "I barely remember my great-grandfather. He's been a ghost to me most of my life." He paused, and stared away for a moment, as if hearing something distant or trying to recall a memory. "Talk about seeing a ghost only started after the fire revealed the wine cellar he'd sealed up. Oh, my God. Jeb was trapped in that room where he died for almost forty years until the fire freed him. He's buried up on the cliff, but he was killed in that sealed-up room. He started trying to communicate with people right after his spirit got set free."

Giving Ruby a frown, he sighed and fell silent.

"The fire released him from a kind of prison, Eli. It was kind of a good thing it happened." Mason touched Eli's hand, squeezing it only once, but firmly. "Have others seen him like I did? Did he visit them in his room?"

Eli shrugged but his fingers wrapped around Mason's hand and held on. "Other people have just mentioned a coldness in the room from time to time or a feeling like they were being watched, but you're the first one he could touch. Maybe it's because you're both artists and more open." Eli jerked his head to one side in a short, tight shudder. "I've never felt anything before like what just happened here."

"Thanks for being here with me." Mason pressed his hand to Eli's until the man looked up at him, then he winked. The small gesture drew a tight smile to Eli's lips and both of them relaxed slightly. Suddenly Mason didn't feel so alone anymore.

Ruby closed the book and gently handed it to Eli. "I think Jeb's ghost is calling to Mason to find his body so it can be buried properly, near the one he truly loved."

Eli accepted the volume, thoughtfully running his hand over the mahogany colored bindings. A family heirloom, taken for granted for another forty years after Eugene had died. One that recorded a new piece of the puzzle that was part of his family's traumatic history.

"I think you're right, Ruby. So let's see to it that he gets a proper final resting place. Eighty-plus years is too long to wait for your lover." Eli winked at Mason through a sad, intimate smile. He stood, pulling Mason along with him and out of the dark, cold, and silent room.

§ § §

Eli notified the authorities. The bones buried on Mourning Cliff, wrapped in canvas and rope, were uncovered under the outcropping of relocated white rock and decades of layered soil.

Personal items found in the body's tattered remaining clothing confirmed that the bones belonged to Jeb Dahl – as if Eli, Mason or Ruby had had any doubt of it. Eli oversaw Jeb's re-burial, laying him to rest in the local cemetery beside Eugene Storm. Eugene had been alone all these years. Eugene's confession was accurate. What had been left of May's crushed and broken body had been retrieved from the base of Mourning Cliff and been cremated, her ashes scattered from Mourning Cliff, only feet from her brother's unacknowledged grave.

As sad as it was, Mason couldn't help thinking that May was the only person to have ever gone over Mourning Cliff twice. Finding humor in the situation lightened some of his lingering unease. He hoped that relocating Jeb's bones had put the anguished spirit to rest and that it had stopped haunting Jeb's old room. He hadn't seen it since the night of the séance, but, to be honest, he wasn't sleeping in Jeb's old room anymore. It had been the best three weeks of vacation he'd ever had. He didn't want it to end. Ever.

But, he needed to know how Eli felt about...well... forever.

Mason rolled over in bed and watched as Eli removed his clothing, marveling at the man's graceful movements and rippling, trim body. Keeping the inn in shape had certainly kept the innkeeper in shape as well.

He felt his erection spring to life and his skin flush at the mere thought of what that body did to him. His gaze moved up to Eli's face, pulled there by the man's sudden stillness. When his glance met Eli's dark eyes, Mason's heart pounded under his ribs cage and his stomach fluttered at the intense stare of loving desire that marked Eli's expression.

Mason's cock jumped and his ass clenched in anticipation and wanting. Making love with Eli was good -- very, very good. The brawny man was tender and rough, considerate and demanding, just when Mason needed him to be all those things. His strong hands and powerful arms caressed, held and manhandled Mason in the best of ways. His fat cock, too, was tender and rough, considerate and demanding just when Mason needed it to be all those things.

Naked and confident, Eli strode toward the bed, gaze pinned to Mason's face, the fire in his eyes leaping higher as he closed the distance.

Mason kicked off the covers and let the man's stare travel down his own equally naked form. He watched Eli smile and raise an eyebrow at the sight of Mason straining, ready cock. He slipped onto the mattress and instantly pulled Mason to him in a passion-fueled embrace.

Long seconds passed as they stared into each other's eyes, love and need dancing in both their faces. A small gasp rolled off Mason's lips and Eli's willing mouth captured it.

Black spots danced before Mason's eyes. He felt the blood pounding through his veins, rising. Then, suddenly Eli released him, and he let slip a whimper of protest at the loss of contact.

Eli rolled over and pinned Josh to the mattress, pressing the length and weight of his entire body into Mason. Mason's breath came in small gasps, filling the space between them. Eli recaptured Mason's lips in a gentler, less demanding kiss, sliding one hand down to grip Mason's hip and one hand up to tangle loosely in his dark hair.

Eli gently parted Mason's legs, settled between them. Mason automatically pulled his knees up on either side of

Eli's hips.

Mason's wrists were caught in a firm grip, his fingers grazing the headboard. Eli slid his hands down Mason's outstretched arms, teasing and caressing each inch of exposed flesh. Mason couldn't stop the moan that escaped his lips, and Eli returned to them with a lingering, deep kiss.

Mason shuddered, rocking his hips up to rub against Eli, forcing cock to cock, sliding hard dick against hard dick, making his own cock slick with pre-cum and eager for more friction. He eagerly reached again for Eli's mouth, exploring it with his tongue, tasting as if it were the first time. He didn't think he'd ever get enough of this strong, quiet, confident man.

Instinctively, a passionate, demanding rhythm began. Mason's hips rocked against the smooth, hard planes of Eli's lower abdomen, growing impatient for more. He ended the kiss, dipped his head down and lavished attention on first one of Eli's taut nipples and then the other until Eli forced his head up to kiss him again.

Those strong hands he loved so much pulled his legs open wider as Eli raised up on his knees. His hand trailed down Mason's chest and abdomen, stroking and touching, exploring and rubbing, forcing Mason's senses to concentrate on each touch and sizzling point of contact. His skin was flushed and he could feel the heat radiate from it, hot, but still no match for the blazing fire from Eli's fingertips.

Pulling his blurry gaze up to meet Eli's sultry expression, Mason's chest ached and his stomach flopped again, thrilled by the love and desire that were so easy to read in Eli's eyes.

Maybe he didn't have to wonder how Eli felt about him. Suddenly, he couldn't hold back any longer. He'd been holding back words, waiting for a perfect time to say them. Instead, the words came tumbling out, the careful rehearsals forgotten.

"I want to see you after this. After I leave. I want to... date?" He gasped as Eli gripped his cock and began a slow, sensuous stroking. The man's eyes never left Mason's face and the tenderness in the caresses never faltered as Mason's rushed, stumbling words and emotions got the better of him. "I think I love you."

Eli smiled and increased the tightness of his grip on Mason's dick. "You think you love me? Only think it?"

Mason groaned and bucked up into the slick, sliding fist. Eli leaned down and licked the crown of Mason's cock as it popped through the clenched hold. Mason gasped and shimmied his hips while Eli's wet tongue explored his slit and hot breath turned the warm spit to cool, wet goodness that dripped over the leaking head.

"Because," Eli continued -- as if Mason wasn't writhing and moaning between his bent thighs -- "I was thinking that I *definitely* love you." He sucked the bulbous crown into his mouth and massaged the flared head with his lips before pulling off Mason's cock with a wet, thrilling hungry sound. "But if you're *only thinking*--"

"God, no! I mean, yesssss." Mason was momentarily distracted as Eli fondling his balls, rolling and tugging gently on the sensitive sac. Mason sighed and surrendered.

Declaring lasting love while making love wasn't the best place time to do it convincingly. But it was going to have to do. " I love you!"

Fists knotted in the sheets at his side, Mason stared up into Eli's face and knew this was the right time, the best time. He could actually see love, love for him and only him, in Eli's eyes. "I was just…I didn't want to say it now…you know while my dick head is doing most of the thinking…but it just rushed out." Realizing how uncertain he sounded, he rushed to add, "I *think* the head on my shoulders got tired of waiting for its turn to be in control."

They had been spending more and more time in bed than out enjoying the bracing autumn and the joys of Ruby's company. Good thing winter was approaching and the days were getting shorter. They had an excuse to go to bed earlier. And they had taken every advantage of the excuse.

Eli laughed out loud and Mason had to join him. The laughter ended in a long, lingering, deep kiss. Eli pulled back enough to look at Mason. "I'm glad that's settled. We'll work on the rest of things later. I *think* this is the important part."

"You think right."

Eli fumbled a condom and lube from the bedside table drawer and tossed it to Mason, who tore open the packet with trembling, eager hands and worked it over his lover's stout dick, layering it with slick, sensual goo. Mason stroked the swollen shaft, loving the feeling of thick power the cock's girth and hardness gave him. His asshole fluttered at the thought of it sliding into him, breaching his outer defenses and filling him, until his ass ached sweetly and his own cock strained with need.

Pulling his knees up, Mason exposed his opening to Eli's hands and ravenous gaze. Mason couldn't decide which one made him hotter -- the Eli that touched his body or the Eli that touched his soul.

His lover entered with measured ease, gauging each thrust against Mason's moans and jerky little nods of eager need. Eli's cock hit Mason's prostate and with just an arch of his back or a twist of his hips, he could ignite bursts of white light behind Mason's eyes and send pleasure to ripping along his nerve endings.

Mason fumbled for Eli's hands, gripping their wrists as Eli supported himself on them. He felt bound to Eli, destined to be here. He felt full again, real.

Eli maintained a slow, steady rhythm of deep, powerful thrusts, every loving stroke aimed to rub over his lover's prostate. Mason was reduced to babbling incoherent half sentences and incomprehensible grunted syllables. With each thrust, Eli tried not to press his full weight onto Mason, but Mason gripped his shoulders and pulled him down, wanting to crawl inside the man's skin when he eased back.

As Mason neared his orgasm, Eli sensed his need and intensified his thrusts, stroking deep and slow, striking at Mason's prostate and stretching his opening so that he was battered by burning pleasure both in his ass and deep inside his groin. It was a seesaw of sensation that had yet to fail to send Mason into orbit. His orgasm began to build behind his tightening sac and the rocking rhythm took on an urgent, primal beat. Their orgasms ripped through them, first Mason's, then Eli's close behind.

Both men lay spent and sweaty on the sheets, amidst wrinkles and wet spots. Eli rolled off Mason, disposed of the condom, and pulled the covers over them before he drew his drowsy, pliant lover back into his arms.

Mason sighed and rolled over, spooning up to Eli's chest and planting his ass in Eli's groin. He liked the sensation of the hot, wet, and still half-hard cock against his burning ass. His opening clenched and spasmed, renewing the pleasurable burn, the burn of being filled and stretched.

An arm dropped around his waist and hot breath whispered over his neck. "*Think* you can deal with this on a regular basis, lover boy?"

"Yes. For once, both my heads are in agreement." Mason reached up and laced his fingers through the fingers of the strong hand on his waist. "I *think* this will work out."

Shadows in Time

"Yesterday upon the stair, I saw a man who wasn't there.

He wasn't there again today. I wish that he would go away."

Nursery Rhyme

Boston

1760

"Shall I take you on the floor tonight? Like a stable mare? What do you say, my boy? Nothing?"

Williams chuckled softly, the harsh sound swallowed up by the thick velvet curtains and heavy bed chamber furniture. He wait a few seconds for his lover's reply then roughly gripped the much younger man's chin, forcing the smooth, angelic face upward. Even so, Neal refused to raise his gaze. Judge Williams pushed Neal's face away with a sharp slap.

"It's just was well. It is not like your preference is of any concern to me."

Contempt always brought such a delicious flush to the boy's fine-boned cheeks. This time was not any different. Williams savored the sweetness of success while he watched Neal try not to squirm. Williams took advantage of the moment to run his hands over Neal's upper arms and shoulders, admiring the trim, firm muscles, the hallmark of a silversmith. They were even more attractive when spread wide and lashed to the foot board of Williams' bed as they were now. Neal's slender body naked and on display for his pleasure as Williams sat on a plush stool in front of the young man, admiring and playing. The long hours Neal spent working metal into delicate wares for his father's silver shop showed. Williams appreciated every curve under the pale skin.

He especially admired the slight curve of hard flesh

jutting up from between Neal's thighs. The color was a tantalizing shade of rose, the length just right to fit in the grasp of his hand, the width slim like the body that claimed it as its own. Though it looked thicker now than normal, the tight bands of the hair tie Williams had torn from Neal's dark wavy locks wrapped securely along its length, ensuring the lad stayed hard and wanting until Williams had what he wanted. Maybe even longer.

Grabbing Neal by the hips, Williams pulled him closer, unbalancing him slightly, forcing Neal's arms back as his wrists remained tied to the foot board. His young lover said nothing until Williams slowly lapped at the swollen crown of Neal's cock, his fingers digging into the lean flesh of Neal's buttocks, his stare fixed on Neal's averted gaze. Even then, a gasp was his only reward. It was infuriating that the boy continued to fight him after all these months. He knew what was required of him and yet he fought, embarrassment and shame ruling over reason and prudent decisions.

"Let me hear you say it, boy." He let his fingernails dig a little deeper, not enough to draw blood but enough to leave a reminder of what disobedience could bring.

"*Look* at me and say it."

He watched the convulsive bob in Neal's throat as he swallowed down the words, marveling at the graceful lines of muscle and flesh that led to the square, beautiful, clenched jaw. He rubbed his own stubbled chin over the bound, glistening cock pointed at his face, delighting in the startled jerk of Neal's hips that unintentionally forced it harder against his prickly cheek.

Ah, the eager slide of hot, weeping flesh against his own. He never tired of it even after four decades of life. He could barely wait to possess this passionate young buck, possess him completely, permanently. Neal's future would be *his* future. Whether the boy wanted it or not.

Williams edged forward on the stool, forcing his knees between Neal's spread thighs. He released his hold on the firm buttocks, bringing both his hands to caress and fondle Neal's groin, cupping his sac then teasing the crease behind it. His fingers were dry but that didn't stop him from exploring and breaching the tight opening to Neal's body with one finger. Neal squirmed and shifted at the sudden penetration. Williams used the movement to go deeper. When he could curl his finger forward and touch a hard bead of flesh he stopped and worried the knot.

Neal curled his toes into the thick weave, visibly tensing his body. Williams knew he was steeling himself against the next touch from his "lover's" groping hand. Yet even as the young man burned with embarrassment and revulsion, his cock betrayed him, hard and weeping, yearning for attention. This was everything Williams loved about seducing naïve young lovers, so beautiful and eager.

Soft gasps and shallow pants filled the silence but Neal still wouldn't speak. Williams bent forward so his lips touched the bobbing cock. He exhaled, letting hot moist air mingle with the drops of cream pooling in the folds of the lengthened foreskin, the tiny slit on the smooth globe under it peeking out.

"What do you think my servants will say come morn when they find you here naked and tied to the bed, cock bound and weeping, as you are now? They know better than to blaspheme my reputation or they will find their worthless hides locked away in chains in prison."

Williams reached up with his free hand, twisting Neal's chin until their gazes finally met. Once gained, he held Neal's gaze with the force of his own harsh stare. Without breaking the line of sight he pulled Neal's cock so he could push down the foreskin and suck softly as the newly exposed head.

Neal grunted, a choked sob swallowed down before it fully escaped.

Williams smiled. "But I dare say, you will not be so lucky, young sir." His smile faded and his eyes narrowed. "Say it." Without waiting for Neal to respond, Williams stilled his finger still deep inside Neal's ass as he licked at a few of strips of cock flesh bulging out between the crisscrossed ribbon. The heat and taste almost made him close his eyes in delight.

Neal's face was the color of pale tea roses, a sheen of sweat giving his skin an unearthly glow, like a distraught angel. His china blue eyes were half-lidded with lust, his mouth parted, dry lips revived every few seconds with an anxious touch from his tongue. Arms restrained to each side and back, his hips pushed forward, a jutting, uncoordinated rhythm, a primal rutting looking for release. His forehead was furrowed, a few lines marring his smooth complexion, this and his silence the only indications he was struggling against Williams' demands.

Williams sucked the cock to the back of his throat, sliding a second finger into Neal to massage the hidden pleasure spot inside. Neal trembled, droplets of sweat running down his taunt abdomen to disappear in the dark spare nest of hair under Williams' grasping hand.

"I...c-crave the pleasure of you... inside me." Neal had to force himself to speak clearly or risk having to repeat himself. Williams sucked harder and Neal shuddered adding. "I want you to...possess me."

"And?" *It was marvelous how one's body could betray one's inhibitions and social taboos. Manipulations were so much more enjoyable this way, if no less humiliating.*

"We—we were meant...to be together." Neal could barely spit the words out.

"That wasn't so hard, now was it?" Williams moved his fingers in short hard jabs, delving deeper, nudging the small stone of heat in Neal's channel while sucking hard on the head of the swollen cock. It leaked and jumped in his mouth, scraping against teeth and tongue. The sound of Neal's strangled cries were music in his ears.

§ § §

Neal's gaze fastened on the faint ink that stained the pale fingertips from too many years of handling legal documents. They always left Neal feeling dirty no matter how clean the hands really were, each long, bony caress like a quill to parchment, writing unpleasant truth on his weak and wanton flesh.

Why had God made him like this? Weak to the pleasures of the flesh and easy prey for the more cunning lover. But with the shame came unspeakable pleasure

—when his lover decided to grant him it. Neal was less concerned over his lover being a man than he was over the kind of man he had fallen for. Better to face eternal damnation over fornication with a good, loving man than the cruel one that had ensnared him.

"Perchance, tonight I won't take you at all. Just leave you and your pride to wither away from lack of attention."

Williams palmed Neal's cock, the coarse ribbons wrapped tightly around the straining flesh rubbing against the sensitive shaft, forcing the trapped blood to pound in the bulging veins entwined up to the leaking tip. Neal couldn't resist thrusting into the grip again and again, his body crying out for release from the torturous wait.

Each touch brought the stink of unpleasant spices, the ground herbs added to an exotic oil his more experienced partner had specially shipped in from the Caribbean. The smell irritated Neal's nostrils and burned his eyes.

The thick, red oil Williams slathered around Neal's mouth was colder than the room, not even warming to his body temperature. Williams' long-fingered hand slithered down Neal's back to paint his naked ass, sliding between the globes of his backside, leisurely seeking entrance to Neal's taut body a second time. The questing digit found the tight bud and wormed into it, the sudden scrape of fingernail soothed by the glide of slick oil, a relief to the used lining.

Neal grunted at the sudden intrusion, a spark of pleasure stroked by the wiggling, prodding rod igniting the fire in the pit of his bowels. His cock hardened, curving away from his naked body, presenting its modest, hooded length to the spice-tainted air. He shuffle his feet awkwardly further apart so he could remain standing the way Williams insisted he did, feet planted on the center of the weird symbol in the middle of the bedroom rug. It was the same symbol the other man wore around his neck, the pattern burned into the fabric pouch that hung from a sturdy ribbon. The game had been going on for months. Neal knew what was expected of him. So much so that it was ritual by now. And he knew the consequences if he didn't play his part.

He stared down at the foreign mark, trying hard not to imagine a stiff manhood or a licking tongue in the curved strokes. Williams had no intention of giving him any sexual release soon, and wild imaginings only made the wait more agonizing.

Shame burned his face, heating radiating from his cheeks hard enough to make his eyes water. He let the rising buzz of humiliation in his ears drown out his partner's nasal words, the eerie, sing-song chant hanging in the air unanswered.

Neal knew his silence didn't matter to Judge Williams, the pompous Boston barrister actually thought it was his due; that all should bow down and be respectful in his presence. Neal had quickly learned the best way to play to the man's weaknesses in ego and physical desires. It had taken time but Neal finally saw the older man for who and what he truly was.

There *had* to be a way out. No matter what it took.

§ § §

"Move swiftly, child. That worm of a man is (dialect) gone to a meeting at the tavern, but I never know when he'll see fit to return. If he catches you here now, he'll burn us both. Hurry, child!"

The sound of passing horse's hooves clatter on the cobblestones echoed faintly down the narrow alley he used to reach the back door. The falling snow muffled his much lighter steps, the stench from the emptied chamber pots thrown out in the street stronger here, lessening the amount of foot traffic and prying eyes.

Ayana's hushed words ran together, heavy and exotic, her Jamaican accent painting blue oceans, warm breezes and lazy sun-drenched days for Neal Clifton like they always had despite the woman's current tense insistence. Neal winced when the housekeeper's hard, bony grip squeezed his arm as she pulled him out of the lightly falling snow and into the warmth of the Judge's small kitchen.

"I know, Ayana." Neal clasped his own chilled hand over hers, returning the comforting touch. She was small in stature, her skin smooth and clear like a petite bronzed sculptures in his father's study. She was a beautiful woman, large dark eyes, coal black hair, and a full-lipped, expressive mouth under high, sharp cheekbones off set by her worn but clean white neckerchief. It framed her neck and face beautifully. Neal could see why she had been considered a royal captive, why Williams had needed to possess her whatever the cost—to her or to her people.

"I'm not sure but I think someone saw me. From the Abbot house next door. Coming around to the alley." He resisted the urge to flee before it was too late.

"Then you must hurry." The warmth of the room pushed the chill away from his back as she urged the door closed. The clink of the door blocked out the outside world of prying eyes and accusing fingers. In the sudden silent of the small, comfortable room his nerves calmed and his courage returned.

"I wasn't to leave town for three more days."

"The time is right now, child. The spirits do not lie."

"Then I'll leave tonight. I'll send a message to father to follow as originally planned so he'll be less inclined to suspect a problem. The transfer of the business back to Philadelphia is almost completed." He had lived his whole life in Boston but a change was needed if his was to have a decent life. He glanced anxiously toward the upstairs chambers. "I have to say, with the latest turn of events, I'm no longer reluctant to go."

Philadelphia was his father's place of birth, but Neal had spent little time there. When his father told Neal he had begun arrangements to return to the Pennsylvanian town five years after his mother's death, it seemed natural. But Neal has been surprised by the plan to merge businesses with a fellow silversmith of equal reputation. Surprised but too distracted by his own troubles to pay much regard to most of what his father told him about the new business plan and their new partner.

After years of working as his father's apprentice, Neal was an excellent silversmith but his real talent lay in the business aspects. He had a head for figures and a natural charm and wit when dealing with people, both customers and business associates. It now offered him a legitimate opportunity to leave Boston. Impulsive as always, Neal leaped at the chance to escape his present situation without further thought.

"I know it was unspeakable of me to ask you to do this but I couldn't think of any other way." Betrayed by his lover, the fine upstanding Judge Martin Williams, Neal's friendship with Ayana, Williams' indentured servant, remained intact, the two of them bound together against one evil.

"I know, child. I know. You must not let him keep *anything* that ties you to him." Her dark eyes were like a fierce storm at night, full of power and anger. "If I could get back what he took from me all those years ago I would send his black spirit to the other side of the darkness and never let his filthy soul find peace!"

If anyone understood what a cruel and abusive man the Judge really was beneath his public mask of respectability and moral righteousness it was this proud and defiant woman, forced into service for over a decade, treated no better than the lowliest slave.

Neal knew Williams had some mysterious, unspoken power over Ayana. Whenever Neal had shown too much curiosity about the subject Williams would only give a randy smirk. Neal was certain she had suffered in the Judge's bedchamber, as well as in his household service, at one time.

And Neal knew all about the Judge's bed these last few months. At first they had been deliriously wonderful times, but Williams' true character soon emerged, and Neal realized what a precarious position he had put himself and his family in. He'd been a fool. Now he was here to correct the grave error his naïve heart had made.

"I only wish you could, Ayana. Unmerciful as it is, I *do* wish it after what he's done! I should have listened to you from the beginning. I was blinded by what I thought was love."

"That man knows nothing of love!" Ayana spat on the floor mumbling a few words Neal didn't understand but recognized as her native tongue. It sounded dark and ominous, curses being brought up from hell. "He is the devil's servant. With *no* heart. The only soul he owns belongs to another! Evil! Evil lives in this house, child, evil and darkness!"

The intensity of venom in Ayana's usually gentle, exotic, sing-song voice startled him. It spurred his desire to do what needed to be done and be gone from this house once and for all. Neal gently disengaged her grasp to stride through the kitchen and into the hallway. He was suddenly anxious to be gone from this place once and for all.

His gaze lingering on the small animal bones scattered on the floor by the hearth. Strangely, Williams had encouraged Ayana to keep her heathen cultural beliefs alive, reveling in the exotic, mystical rituals. She clung to them in a fanatical manner Neal wasn't quite comfortable with. She had refused to let Neal into the house until the spirits and mystic signs had told her the time was right. Apparently, the bones favored him this evening.

The bones appeared to vibrate as he walked by them sending a chill through his chest, spurring him to walk faster. He took the staircase two treads at a time, the hallway to Williams' chambers at a trot. Ayana followed, her pace slower but just as anxious, lit candle in hand.

Neal threw open the door and moved into the familiar room with the ease that spoke of many hours spent in the plush surroundings. Too many hours that created too many detailed memories. Memories that echoed off the cold walls to hammer accusingly at Neal. Gone was the pleasure he had first discovered here. Passion and adoration had turned to bitter guilt and shame.

"He keeps his personal papers this drawer." Neal moved to the ornate desk in the corner of the room and lit a another candle off Ayana's flame. Light splashed across the cluttered surface and shadows danced on the walls like demons guarding the gates of hell. The room was chilled, smelling of burnt ash and spices. Neal yanked on the upper drawer of the desk, frustrated but not surprised when it didn't budge.

"The key would be best, but he never takes it off. Even when he's…" Neal paused, embarrassed though he knew Ayana was aware of the things that happened in this room between Williams and himself, "…unclothed." He was surprised by how much disgust there was in his voice. Disgust for the Judge's offensive behaviors but mostly for his own foolhardy actions. He was responsible for the trouble he found himself in.

Ayana touched his arm, her voice low and soft. "You are young, Neal. You think with a young man's heart. A heart that looks at life with passion and love. Do not let this deceiver change your heart. I know of his charms and sly ways." She tapped Neal's chest, a soothing, maternal pat of acceptance. "Yours is a good heart, child. There will be others to share it with, even if your lovers are not ordinary choices."

She nodded a small knowing smile on her full, brown lips. She traced the curve of his cheek and jaw with a tenderness that brought tears to his eyes. If she had been allowed the life she had been meant to have, Ayana would have been a wonderful mother in Neal's estimation. "Love is love and it is meant to be shared. You will find another who deserves your heart. A better man than Judge Martin Williams!"

"That shouldn't be too hard considering the Judge's character, but I doubt it, Ayana. After this, my 'choices' must remain secret, buried where no one can use them against me again. I can never trust another not to betray me. Never. There is too much to lose. My father would never recover from the shock. He is all the family I have left to me. I can't let Williams take that away from me as well."

A letter opener lay to one side on the desktop, its gleaming metal bright and inviting in the glow of the candle light. Neal jabbed it into the lock space and forced the metal to give under the full weight of his slight frame. The drawer cracked and splintered under the pressure. Neal yanked it open. Ayana touched his arm but said nothing. Neal paused, concern for her twisting his inside into knots. She would be here to bear the Judge's wrath at the drawer's destruction, not he.

Ayana shook her head. "Broken lock or not, once he discovers them missing he'll know who took them. Do not fear for my safety, child. I will survive as I have done all this years."

"I'm sorry, Ayana. The last thing I want is for him to hurt you because of me."

"Hush and hurry before he returns and we both feel his displeasure."

Neal stared into her fathomless black eyes and wondered for the hundredth time how this woman had remained so goodhearted while withstanding the isolation and humiliation Williams forced on her. He knew he could not have tolerated it. A few short weeks on the Judge's leash and he was willing to do anything to escape. Including thievery.

Pushing a few loose parchments aside, Neal retrieved a slim bundle of letters out of the back of the drawer. They were wrapped in dark red ribbon, the one Neal had used to tie back his wavy brown hair the last night Williams had seduced him.

Williams had used it to bind his hands over his head the second night they spent together. More recently it had been tied around his shaft while Williams teased and tortured him until he begged for release. Dark stains marred the ribbon, mute testament to his eventual relief. He could feel the burn of shame on his fair skin and the buzz of humiliation in his ears forcing him to turn his back until he could regain control. He had even cut his hair shorter after his last night so as to no longer need to wear a hair tie.

Before he regained his composure, the air in the room shifted and a deep, mocking voice chilled his flesh and froze his heart.

"Stealing your love letters, as passionate and revealing as they are, will hardly be worth the thievery charge, if I still have your thoughtful and rather damning gift, don't you think, Neal, my dear boy?" That nasal, condescending tone rippled over Neal like tainted honey, thick, sweet -- suffocating. Words stuck in his throat like flies.

"Mercy!" Ayana surprised gasp made Neal spin around to face his tormentor head on, sliding the bundle under his waistcoat before he turned.

Williams had the advantage of several inches of height over Neal, his wide shoulders shrugged in an insolent pose of privilege and vague distaste. The sharp angles of his ruddy face appeared more pronounced in the ineffectual candlelight. A sheen of sweat glistened on his forehead, his skin color paler than usual. Neal hoped it was because the Judge had been caught off guard but he knew that outwitting the sly, older man wasn't even a possibility.

Williams' dabbed at his lips with a folded pocket handkerchief, keeping it in his hand to pat deliberately at his face again before speaking, his words slightly hesitant and stilted. "I greatly doubt your father's reputation will hold up under the scandal."

"You won't show them to anyone." Neal's chest tightened. He knew Williams was politically connected enough to escape prosecution but it was all he had. "You'd ruin yourself as well!"

Williams abruptly stepped closer. Ayana held her ground nearby, but Neal jerked back, then stumbled, brought up short by the desk. His resolve to follow through on this mission was still strong, but he was fearful of the power and rage the other man wielded. He'd felt the weight of that rage too often these last few weeks.

The desk candle shuddered sending the shadows into a frenzied riot before it stilled. Their dark grasping fingers retreated but not before Neal felt their empty chill tug at his flesh.

Face uncharacteristically gray like the muted edges of the gloomy room, Williams ran his palm down Neal's face, a tender touch that turned to a grip of iron on his jaw when he tried to flinch away. "You are so young, sweet Neal, all innocent wonder in those wide blue eyes." Williams gave a leering sneer, his heavy lidded eyes tight with scorn. "Even now that you are not so innocent anymore."

Neal's jaw ached with the force of the hold but he refused to look away. A long finger slid back and forth over his closed lips as if Williams was wagging an accusing finger at a naughty child. Williams' hand tightened painfully on Neal's chin then disappeared to return a second later as a vicious backhand slap. The force would have sent him reeling if he hadn't been trapped between the desk and Williams' larger frame.

From the corner of his momentarily blurred vision he saw Ayana step forward as if to intercede.

William ground out a low, menacing command without turning her way. "Stay yourself, woman. Come near me and you will lose something even more precious than what the boy will."

Ayana spit at Williams' feet, her dark eyes searching his face, a small smile forming slowly on her lips. "I hope the evil you bartered with so many years ago is eating away your black, merciless soul. I can smell it oozing out of your skin. I pray it has a full meal!" She mumbled a few words in her native tongue, rattling the strings of beads and bones she wore around her neck.

One hand nursing his stinging face, Neal brought his other arm up to stop her, but she was already backing away to the edge of the room. He knew he would bear bruises from this confrontation, but he wouldn't be responsible for her sharing the abuse because she wanted to protect him.

"Ever the *chivalrous* gentleman." The scorn was palpable. Williams grabbed Neal by the hair then thrust him away, his fingers suddenly gripping the front of his own chest as he stepped back, pain etched on his face. Ayana and Neal made small, startled noises, both unused to seeing the powerful man hesitate for any reason. Williams let out a hollow chuckle.

"Merely indigestion. Don't squeal with triumph yet, Ayana. No doubt spoiled meat in the pies at the tavern." With an obvious effort to compose himself, Williams patted his cloth to his neck and took a deep breath through clenched teeth. It gave his voice a raw, gritty quality that was chilling. "But I doubt public opinion will be swayed by good manners and a sweet face. In fact, it will probably be your undoing. An angelic face used to try to seduce an older man against his wishes in to the devil's clutches. Unsuccessfully, of course, but others will see how I could be tempted by such a beautiful but immoral, libidinous young man."

The sneer of contempt made Neal nauseous. "My

father is…aware of my…unconventional desire in bed partners."

"Yes, no doubt, considering his own randy youth. But does he want the world to know of it as well?"

How could he have ever seen this man as anything else than a monster? "Please, Martin, don't do this!"

"Your actions today leave me no recourse, my boy. Conspiracy with my maid. Thievery." Williams stopped to struggle for a breath. "Your father, the most respected silversmith in Boston, will know his only son –and heir to his sizable fortune-- to be guilty of trying to seduce a respected member of the legal system to engage in a disreputable behavior." Williams' eyes squinted as if he were in pain, his complexion more ashen that before. "What do you think that will do to his current plans to combine his business with that of Wade House? More importantly, what will Wade House think of it?" He paused, letting all the complications sink into Neal's brain. "Unless…"

"Unless what?" If there was a solution to this, a way out without more shame and ruin, Neal needed to hear it.

"Unless you agree to everything and anything I demand. Whenever I demand it of you, inside this bedroom and out of it." Williams leaned against the high, carved footboard in a confident pose but looked suspiciously as if the man needed the support to stand upright.

"Do not listen, Neal." Ayana trembled, her fingers reaching out to Neal as if to snatch him away from Williams' influence. "He weaves more lies with each word from his forked tongue! He will make you his slave as he did me. Take your very soul. You do not want this." Her nails dug into the palms of her hands so hard Neal could see the creases left behind when she unclenched them again. "Trust me, child. Ruin is better than this living hell."

Neal stared at Williams, taking in the satisfied smirk and the expectant tilt of head as he waited for Neal to break under the magnitude of trouble the judge could create for him. Something inside of Neal unfurled and rose up in his chest. He had to work to push the words past the emptiness it left in its place. He could not disgrace his family name. He'd beg if he had to.

"You've taken so much from me already, Martin – all joy in life, my pride, and my self-respect." It was a losing battle to keep the moisture from blurring his vision but he consoled himself that no tear was actually shed before this devil.

"That is the cost of my silence and protection. Take it or not. The choice is yours." He dragged a smug glance up Neal's slender body. "After all, I'm not asking for anything more than you have already given me."

"You mean *taken*. You used me! Used my own untried wants and desires to blind me to your true nature. I was naïve and inexperienced, eager to accommodate a worldly man of professed good standing to introduce me to the ways of knowing another man. Something I had craved but didn't know how to express." He clenched a fist and pounded the desktop. "I had no idea how ruthless and cruel a man you were until now."

Suddenly it all seemed nightmarish and grotesque.

Gone was any sense of joy he had experienced the first few times Williams had pleasured him. The weight of the letters tucked into his waistcoat felt like the chains lashed to a drowning man. This needed to end.

Neal straightened and backed a few steps toward the doorway and Ayana. "I have the letters back. You can't prove anything."

"Ah, yes, but you are forgetting something. I still have the most damning piece of evidence of your attempts to persuade me into sin." Williams pulled a gold watch from his waistcoat pocket and tossed it playfully in the air before opening it. He squinted at the inside lid, reading aloud in a dramatically infatuated stage whisper. "*M.W. Let others not Judge our love, Neal.*"

He waved it slowly through the air as if showing the world the traitorous words of love Neal has foolishly engraved on the watch himself. "I especially like the way you capitalized 'Judge'. Such an affecting turn of phrase, don't you think? So cleverly fraught with double meanings. I'm sure the court will be properly impressed by your implicit declaration of love." Williams' smile was strained and thin lipped. Neal wasn't sure if it was irony or pain that gave it a twisted, pinched effect. "Love for a *man*. How impulsive of you, my sweet, pathetic..." His eyes had a faintly wild look in them but he gave Neal another dismissive sneer, clutched the open watch roughly to his chest and slowly let the word drip off his now gray lips. "...*catamite*. Or now that I'm paying for your place in my bed, I wonder, does that make you a prostitute instead?"

"Damn you, you bastard!" Neal lunged for the watch but Williams effectively removed it from his reach, toppling over to the floor. The Judge landed face down, both arms and the watch pinned under him.

Neal stood frozen in place not knowing whether to run while Williams no longer blocked his exit or try to wrestle the watch from the man.

Williams moaned and rolled over to his back. His hands scrabbled at his neck, tearing away his stock and under it, the button to his shirt's neck slit. His eyes were wide open, clear and focused on Neal's face. Pain twisted at his thin lips, a rasping breath rattled in his throat so low and feral Neal couldn't believe it came from a man.

Torn between fleeing and giving aid, Neal's sense of right and wrong pushed him to drop to his knees beside Williams. His gaze darted between the judge's ashen face to carpet, searching for the damning pocket watch.

"I can't understand what he is saying." Neal leaned closer. Under the side of Williams' body lay his watch, the hinge slightly twisted, the face open, the hands ticking away the second of Neal's life. "Maybe he is trying to ask for forgiveness."

"Do not touch him! He is trying to call the dark ones. Trying to summon the power of life after death. He needs a vessel to house his rotten soul in so it isn't taken to the afterlife. Stay back!" Ayana approached Williams' side but stopped short of touching him, instead choosing to kneel several feet away on the thick carpet. On hands and knees, she stared at Williams, watching his hands work a thin ribbon that was around his neck out from under shirt with clumsy fingers, nail beds tinged with blue. Her face lost the rich shade of bronze Neal has always thought of as being more beautiful than the richest brown velvet, her expression one of horror. "Stop him!"

"What?" As much as he wanted the watch, he couldn't bring himself to lean over Williams and grab it. Not while the man's hands still clawed at his own throat, snarling his fingers in the tangle of ribbons and strings that decorated his neck. A black pouch, the desk key and gold ring hung from separate strands. Neal saw them every time he had been bedded by the man. But the judge had never revealed their contents or purpose no matter how many times Neal had asked. Nor did he ever take them off.

"Stop his hands." Ayana grabbed at the air in a frustrated parody of Williams' gestures, every fiber of her being showing a need to dig her nails into the man's flesh. "I cannot touch him while it remains in his possession!"

"What? While what remains?"

"My amulet!" If it was possible to screech in a whisper, Ayana succeeded at it. "The pouch! Take it from him. He must not have its power at his command! If he opens the gates to the darkness we will never be rid of his black soul."

None of this made sense to Neal, he didn't even believe it, but his next protest died unspoken as Williams suddenly stopped all movement. His hands rested on his still chest, the black pouch clenched in his left palm, and his face slack, eyes mercifully closed. The rattle from his lungs died away with a sudden puff of breath that already smelled of death.

Neal traded a horrified, shamefully relieved glance with Ayana then choked on his next breath as a bold knock on the front door echoed up the staircase. Ayana jumped to her feet, eyes lit with a dark, almost insane fear. Neal started to rise but she stayed him with a curt command.

"Stay! Take what you came for quickly! I have much to tell you. My pouch must stay in your possession. Give it only to me!" Her steps quick and silent, she ran to the doorway. "I will send the caller away and return. Make no sound!" With that she was gone.

Neal heard the front door open and the muffled sound of insistent voices, one Ayana's and two males. He couldn't afford to waste time. The Judge's associates treated Ayana as if she barely existed. He knew she would be unable to detain them long if they were insistent on coming in to wait.

Time was ticking away.

The watch lay tucked slightly under the man's flaccid body. Neal stared at the ashen face, seeing none of the wit and charm he had been attracted to, none of the generosity or kindness Williams had pretended to possess in the beginning of their relationship. Nothing of the man he had thought he loved. It had all been a cruel lie, a deception for control and personal gain. Williams had made a mockery of Neal's emotions.

The voices below became clearer, the callers unwilling to be turned away. Unable to tear his gaze away from Williams' lifeless face, Neal leaned over the body to pluck the watch off the ground. The twisted lid clicked closed in his hand. The usual crisp ring of metal to metal was missing, the bent edge leaving a gap in the outer seam. His fingers wrapped around the closed shell, but as he pulled back, cold, strong hands sunk into his shirt and held him in place. Williams' eyes sprung open, the pupils dilated so wide Neal felt like he was staring into an abyss.

"Lord have mercy!" Neal's whispered oath thundered in his ears. Absolute terror gripped his throat. The watch fell from his nerveless hand to land on Williams' chest just above his heart, gleaming gold against too pale flesh.

Neal grasped Williams' clawing fingers, trying to force them open. Williams' strength bested Neal on an ordinary day but now the judge seemed to have the power of three men. He yanked Neal closer, drawing Neal to his face.

Williams' mouth contorted, his cold lips brushing Neal's, his whispered words foreign and curt. There was a rhythm to them that repeated again and again, a chant spoken in a raw broken voice Neal didn't recognize as belonging to Williams, despite witnessing it.

The room grew colder and the shadows seemed to move on their own, creeping closer, long gray talons reaching out from the darkness to push the light from the room. They had a life of their own. Neal felt as if they were reaching for him. A white mist flowed from the judge's mumbling lips, pouring around his mouth to cover his cheeks and eyes, a mask of swirling vapor that hid Williams' human features turning them into a caricature of death. The mass moved as if blown by an unseen wind, forming tentacles that clawed at Neal's lips seeking entry to his body. Its touch brought sharp stinging pain as if he was being stung by insects.

Panic seized Neal unlike any he had even experience. He tore at the frozen fingers holding him down, his frantic efforts finally managing to rip his shirt free. His hands came away with the small black pouch that had been in Williams' hand as well, the thin, worn ribbon breaking under the strain. Neal fell back, hitting his head on the leg of the desk when he landed.

Suddenly the judge went rigid, his eyes blank, dark voids. The mist rose in the air, spinning like a directionless top, uncertain where to find refuge.

It was terrifying but at least the rising chant had stopped. More terrifying were the voices from below. They were growing closer, Ayana's insistent tones respectfully but unsuccessfully trying to divert the callers.

His vision blurred for a moment, the blow on the desk leg harsh to his unprotected temple. In the haze that clouded his eyesight, the room swirled with a white mist. It flew at him. He instinctively raised his hand to his mouth to prevent it from clawing at his face again. The black pouch in his palm brushed his lips, the fabric soft and warm. It made him think of one of Ayana's comforting touches after a cruel night spent with the judge.

The vapor whirled and backed away from Neal to return to Williams' body. It lingered by his gaping, lifeless mouth, then reared up to the height of a man, its ghostly veil transformed into a hideous gray face of rotten flesh and exposed bone. As unnatural as it was, Neal could still see Williams' resemblance in the ghastly form. Its false mouth gaped open wide, tattered lips twisted in what Neal imagined to be a soundless scream. Then the visage sunk down low over the judge's body to disappear under the man's open shirt.

Neal stared at the dead man, disbelieving what his senses told him. This couldn't be real. Ayana believed in such things but God-fearing, civilized men did not. It was shock at the judge's death, terror over being exposed, and the blow to his head that brought these nightmarish visions before him. By the time Neal was back on his feet the room was occupied by nothing but shimmering shadows and flickering candlelight. Reality was back in place. Only the hammering of his heartbeat at his wounded temple and the stinging of his lips told him otherwise.

The fear of discovery was more overwhelming than any fear he retained of the dead man. He plunged his hand under Williams' open neck slit. The watch was hard and real under his touch. He snatched it away and jumped back from the body. Shoving both it and the pouch into his jacket pocket, Neal raced to the bed chamber door and quickly but silently strode to the servants staircase at the end of the hall. Once he made it safely to the kitchen he listened in the hallway, hidden by the shadows.

"He said not to disturb him. He was not feeling well, sir."

The voice of Jonathan Webster carried loud and clear, overriding Ayana's objections. "We understand that, woman. We were with him at the tavern when he took ill."

The more placating tone of George Crisp, a barrister like Webster, smoothed over Webster's more condescending approach. "Mr. Webster and I are here to inquire about his current health. Martin was so unsteady when we parted he couldn't even get his watch into his pocket properly. Your neighbor says he thought a friend of the judge's came by as well. If he's up for young Mr.

Clifton's company he won't mind seeing us."

"I sent Mr. Clifton away. The judge wished to be left alone."

"I see. You do look out for the Judge but," He was more polite but also firmer, "we insist."

There was silence then Ayana's strained voice carried more clearly to Neal's hiding space as he watched her turn toward the back hall where lead to the kitchen. "As you wish, sirs. He retired to his chambers when he arrived home. It's at the top of the stairs." Ayana glanced to the darkened hallway and at Neal as if she could see him standing in the shadows. "I was making him tea. I should go finish."

"Nonsense, woman." Webster herded her up the stairs in front of them. "Announce us! My God, after ten years one would think a servant, even one from a heathen country, could learn proper manners!"

Neal stepped back into dim of the kitchen. This would be his only chance to escape unseen. He would send word to Ayana, keep her trinket safe with him until he could come back to give it to her. It was a pouch of herbs and bones as far as he could tell. If she had survived Williams having it for so long, what harm could a few more weeks do? She would understand. If he were caught here, they would know she had lied to them.

At the back door, he edged it open as quietly as possible, pleased to see the evening light had extinguished. The courtyard was wrapped in a shroud of darkness that would cover his movements from prying eyes. Footprints in the snow would support Ayana's claim he had been there and gone, the still falling snow making it impossible to tell when they had been made if they didn't discover them soon. With luck, no one would be aware of the truth.

It took him extra time to maneuver through the side streets to the place where he'd left his horse. It was wiser to wait until morning to travel but Neal needed to put distance between himself and this place. Needed time to think things through. He'd made a mess of things. Allowed lust and desire to put him in a dangerous position with a man who cared only about using him as Williams used everyone.

He was worried about leaving Ayana there alone to handle things. If Williams' death wasn't accepted for the natural demise it truly was she would be a suspect. He was keenly aware she was a strong, clever woman. A woman more concerned that Neal remove her trinket from Williams' possession than his unexpected death. Which was ridiculous. With Williams dead, she *was* a free woman, the pouch had nothing to do with it.

Still…

He slipped his hand into his pocket and fingered the crude bag before taking it out. On impulse, he tied a knot in the broken ribbon and slipped it over his head and under his own shirt. When it touched his skin he felt oddly comforted by it. Ayana's gentle, exotic voice whispered in his head "be strong, child, be strong", a phrase she had spoken many times to him in the last few humiliating weeks. She had endured ten years with that monster while Neal had been willing to be branded a thief after only a few weeks under the man's cruel power. Ayana was stronger than any man Neal knew, including Williams.

He slowly retrieved the damning watch from his pocket. The metal was cold and hard against his palm, the uneven edge of the bent cover sharp against his skin. He was a fool to have engraved it. A fool to have given it to Williams. It felt different in his palm — heavier, colder. Touching it now gave him a gathering sense of dread.

Dropping it back in his pocket, Neal decided it was the added guilt and shame it symbolized, the embodiment of a disastrous attempt to find and explore his own identity and needs. He was convinced it was the wrong man not the wrong need that was his error. His parents had taught him that love, a precious and rare thing, couldn't be a sin. No matter what others believed.

He would keep the accursed watch, a reminder of the damage an unwise choice could bring to an unsuspecting heart. Maybe it would keep him from making the same mistake again. He hated to think love was fleeting and there was no such thing as the 'right man', not for *another* man. He wanted to find the right man. But how would he know when he saw him?

An ache pressed up under his breastbone so intense it made Neal swallow hard to try and dislodge it. Unsurprisingly, it didn't work. If anyone would ask, he'd blame the moisture on his face on the melting snowflakes.

§ § §

Philadelphia

"Room's at the top of stairs, last one on the left, Master Clifton, the one your father always uses." Amos Ross poured a pint and handed it off to a waiting customer. He rounded the bar top to shake hands, a sincere grin of welcome on his ruddy face.

Ross was robust and hearty. Not a large man but fit for a man of his apparent age. He had an honest face and a clear eye for a man who serviced ale all day. His grip was firm. The friendly pat on the back Neal's balance slightly off and a stinging hand print behind.

"You've only got half your father's bulk, son. Sorry, boy, I'll have to remember not to rough you like I do him." Ross laughed and lightly rubbed where he'd patted Neal's back. The man's good mood was infectious and Neal had to return the teasing, good-natured grin. He could see why his father had been a lifelong friend.

The Ram's Head Inn was as inviting as the redheaded man's rough, warm handshake. The cozy dining room was filled with animated customers and the pleasant aroma of baked bread filled the air. "Will you be wanting a bit of a supper? I could have the cook save a bowl of her dish."

"No, thank you, Mr. Ross. It's been a long, cold journey. As much as I am enticed by the offer, my father having spoken highly of your cook's skills, I believe I'll just retire for the night. It was…difficult to rest on the road."

Neal's fitful attempts at sleep had been filled with disturbing dreams and night terrors. He'd been jarred awake more than once by a stinging at his lips, the touch of cold fingers on his face, the windblown snow swirling gray to white in a menacing dance before him. He hoped once he arrived at a secure, populated inn, the unnatural terrors would fade.

"Call me Amos, lad. Your father and I have been too close for too long for less."

"Amos it is then, sir."

"Good. The fire's being tended to in your room. It'll take the chill right off your bones, yes it will." Amos relieved Neal of his travel bag and walked to the stairs. They trudged up the narrow staircase, Amos in the lead.

"I would like to wash up before I turn in. Rid myself of a few layers of road dust." Neal ran hand over the light stubble on his face. Memories were making him feel dirtier than any grime from the trip, but freshening up might make it easier to face another night.

"There's a pitcher of hot water in your room." Amos reached the last door at the end of the long hallway. The door was open revealing a large bedchamber, almost as welcoming as Neal's own room back home. Amos nodded at a large white pitcher on a dresser and waved a lad of about six years of age out of the room. "Had the boy take it up when I sent him off to tend the fire. Thought you might like that. Your father always does. "

The walls had been papered in a subtle pattern, cheerful but masculine. A door on the far wall had a barrel lock in place. Neal assumed it was a connecting room. Possibly where his father would stay when he arrived. The tapestry curtains were heavy enough to block out the strongest morning light and the inevitable draft that seeped around the windows of even the finest home. A fire crackled in the grate, small flames in the tinder already lapping at the split logs and coal.

Neal moved to the hearth and let the warmth soak into his legs and hands. "Now I know firsthand why my father always choose your company, Amos. This is like being home. Thank you."

"Jonathon will always have a place in my home. Time and circumstances have never changed that between us."

"I know he values your friendship as well, Amos. The bond between you has been unbreakable despite distance and marriage. And now that mother is gone, I'm pleased he will have your friendship to rely on. His health is not its best. I'm confident your nearness will give him comfort."

Amos set Neal's bag on wooden chair in the corner. He nodded at Neal, accepting the compliment with grace and a pleased grin. "Thank you, lad. We're fortunate to get a second chance to make some more memories. It's an honor to have you here, as well. Though I'm a bit surprised to see you here alone."

The man's humble appreciation of his father made Neal's chest ache. He had never experienced a friendship as dear as these two held. Neal had always preferred the companionship of older men and none of them had time or patience for him. Until Williams.

How could he ever have survived the humiliation and shame in his father's eyes if Williams had succeeded in his plan? His heartbeat faster the mere thought of the judge. Dead or not, the man still terrified Neal.

"He'll follow in a few days. I had completed some personal business earlier than I expected and decided to arrive early. I sent a message to inform him I would meet him here. I'm sure he won't mind."

"Did you have any last minute chats with him?"

"No," Neal fought to keep his voice from trembling with the memories. "I'm afraid my leaving was a bit of a whim. Impatient I suppose."

"Jonathan always said you were an impulsive lad."

Neal was too shaken to do anything other than let the comment go. "Since I will be working closely with Wade House's proprietor, I thought it might be a good idea to meet with our new business associate on my own. I'm to take a more active part in the day to day running of things."

Amos nodded sagely, a look on his ruggedly pleasant face that told Neal he knew more about the elder Clifton's personal and business plans than Neal might. "Peter Wade is a good man. As fine a silversmith as there ever was. Almost as fine as your father. Bit of a loner, that one. Single man and all." Amos' jaw cocked to one side in an indulgent smile. He winked at Neal. "But I'm betting a handsome, fine young man like yourself will be just the thing for him. He suits you. Your father has high hopes you'll agree."

"My father?" The conversation has taken a confusing turn.

"He thinks highly of the man. As do I, lad. We've both known Peter since he was a boy. But you'll see for yourself." He winked again, as if sharing a guarded confidence. It was all wasted on Neal. He had no idea what the man was trying to tell him. "If you'll be wanting a nightcap later, you know where to find me, lad." With a nod and another face-splitting grin, Amos was gone and the door closed.

The room was comfortably furnished with a plush bed, a dresser, and a ornate clothes cupboard. His bag sat on a straight backed wooden chair and by the fireplace were two upholstered sitting chairs done in a dark fabric. It was clean, cozy and warming up nicely. Even apart from his friendship with Amos, Neal could understand why his father's practical side chose this place over the more luxurious accommodations he could easily afford. The elder Clifton never forgot his humble beginnings.

The faint scent of lye mingled with the smell of fresh bread and strong ale that drifted up from the lower level. Neal's stomach rumbled in response to the foods but the bed, with its fresh sheets and thick comforter, spoke louder. He made short work of washing, including shaving the light stubble from his face. He might have waited until the morn but bathing made him feel as if he had removed a part of the troubles he carried with him from Boston. He wished the frightening vision in his dreams would wipe away as easily.

Embers burned low in the hearth. Neal banked the fire for the night. He sank down on the bed in his shirttails with only the glow of dying coals for illumination. The pocket watch lay on the small stand by the bed where he had placed it when he undressed. He automatically reached for it to check the time, but hesitated as he had learned to do these last few days.

What was once meant to be symbol of his heart was now a looming, weighty reminder of how empty his life was — empty and destined to stay that way. He'd been foolish to think a man could love another man and find happiness in it. Any burden or pain the watch now caused him was just, a lesson to be remembered.

And it did cause him considerable unease. Touching it made his hands shake. The flesh that made contact with its cold, hard surface seemed to burn as if he had handled a glowing ember, despite there being no evidence of any wound. Each time he had an illogical need to inspect it, sincerely expecting to find it waterlogged with ice or snow to explain the new heaviness to the metal.

And still it kept perfect time. The graceful, slender hands ticking away in their unhurried rhythm, the face maybe a shade darker as if a shadow lay under the glass. At least he assumed the watch still keep good time. He hadn't been able to force himself to pry open the bent lid and look since retrieving it from Williams' body. But he could hear the steady *tick*, even and strong like a heartbeat encased in gold.

Crawling under the comforter, Neal pulled it high, snuggling down. His hands fell to rest over his heart, the steady thrumming reassuring. His gaze darting right and left, staring into the deepening gloom.

The room grew darker as the embers waned and the once small shadows arched high, rearing up, frightened horses in the moonlight. Blood pounded at his temples, his heartbeat thundering in time to the ticking of the watch beside his head. He strained his hearing, listening for some sound of the people below. But the room was well-placed and no sounds reached him except for the faint rattle of the windowpanes against the gusting winds.

Neal shut his eyes, trying to relax, ignoring the unease that crept across his skin. He shivered, part natural chill, part trepidation. Nights had not gone well since Williams' death.

Turning on his side, he drew his lower legs closer to his body and slipped his fingers under the collar of his shirt for warmth. The thin ribbon of Ayana's amulet tickled his palm flooding his mind with thoughts of the woman, his unlikely friend and confidant.

It plagued him that he had left her alone to sort out the circumstances of the judge's death. Both he and Ayana were blameless, but that didn't mean others would see it that way. By all rights it had been a death by natural causes, no matter how unnatural the events afterward had appeared to be.

A slight wailing sound whispered near Neal's head. He buried his face deeper into the pillow and kept his eyes tightly shut. He had heard it every night since leaving Boston. The wind at the windows. It *had* to be the wind.

The wail rose and fell, never louder than a breathy sigh but with a menacing hiss to it that made Neal's stomach churn. His grip tightened on the ribbon in his hand, fingernails raking his chest. Each time this had happened on the trip, he had forced himself to abandon rest and push on, the gray mist seemingly unable to torture him unless sleep was approaching.

Breath, cold and foul smelling, brushed his cheek, the hand of death caressing his face. The sound tormented him, its singsong rhythm so close to the last words Williams had spoken he was sure it was his mind playing guilty tricks.

Neal was determined not to give into an apparition of his own making this time. But when the fiery stings gnawed at his face trying to pry his lips apart, he couldn't stand the terror a moment longer.

Each night the vision had a more recognizable form. Not human but no longer a shapeless cloud, either. The face was better defined tonight, sharp angles and shallow curves around a slash that could be a mouth. The eyes were empty sockets, dark holes with no spark of life or kindness in them. Jagged claws formed from twisted strands of smoke-like gray pierced his mouth, pulling at his jaw, stabbing his flesh until the pain rivaled a horde of wasps. His heart pounded in his chest, his throat so tight he could barely breathe.

Instinctively his hands flew up, ineffectively fighting off the wisps of smoky talons. His fingers tangled in Ayana's ribbon, the sudden movement pulling the amulet from under his shirt. The small pouch popped into the air then fell back when it reached the end of the ribbon's length around his neck. It landed on Neal's lips with a light slap, the faint scent and taste of exotic spice and rich dirt released from it by the impact.

Neal reached to wipe the fine dust away. He froze, his hand on his mouth, the pouch and its dust the only thing there. The mist had reared up, giving a whispered sound that was closer to a screech than the usual chants.

It swirled around the room again and again, building up speed and power then rushed headlong at Neal.

Neal sealed his hands over his mouth, pouch and dust in his palms and braced himself. At the last minute, he rolled out of the way, landing on the floor on the far side of the bed. Tangled in linen and shirttails, he lay there listening and waiting. When nothing happened except his teeth chattering from the cold, he slowly regained his feet. The room was empty, undisturbed except for the watch. It lay on the bed as if it had been knocked from the stand. Neal quickly grabbed it and closed it in the table's drawer.

He was sure he would get no sleep again this night. It took several attempts for him to settle back in bed, but the release of tension and a nearly sleepless week of travel took its toll. The taste of spice on his lips and tongue were oddly comforting, like his mother's pudding when she was alive. Reassuring.

His last thoughts were of Ayana, her precious amulet and his failing mental state. If this was all just his becoming unbalanced with guilt, it was going to be a rapid decline. He wouldn't have to worry about finding happiness.

§ § §

The city bustled with energy undaunted by the second snowfall in as many days. The streets were frozen, cobblestones slick with snow and ice packed solid by carriage wheels and hooves. The thick, large flakes gave the busy street sounds a muffled grace.

Glancing expectantly up the lane, Peter Wade swept the snow from the stoop of his storefront. As much as he respected, admired and even liked John Clifton, he was nervous. This arrangement was far from ordinary.

"I imagined Neal Clifton to be made from the same cloth as his father, Amos? Thick limbed and heavyset?"

Amos Ross chuckled and shook his head. "I don't want to spoil the surprise." They entered the shop.

Peter poked a bit, wanting more to go on from this wild plan. "Jonathon is easy company for a gentleman of such distinguished reputation and wealth. We have agreeable viewpoints, but his son is said to have a keen head for figures. I'm not sure a squinty-eyed clerk is best suited to my temperament."

"You're an impatient for a man ending his third decade, Peter Wade. And one who can't afford to be passing up an opportunity of this kind. Your financial future in business will be set as well as an end to the lonely days and nights I know you're enduring. So buck up, man. I've never know you to walk away from a challenge. Don't make this one your first."

"My skill with the metal is on equal standing with the fine Clifton Silver's goods." Picking up the piece he had finished last evening, he examined the joining to see if it would benefit from another polishing. "But you know I lack an interest in the more practical end of business."

"Which is way this is a reasonable end to it."

"I feel like the nervous groom in an arranged marriage."

"That's because you are, man! Trust me. Jonathon knows what he's doing. He knows his son and he knows you. Better than your own mother did." Amos gave Peter the look that said it all. "The three of us know the reason you're still a bachelor. Same reason I am. If Jonathon hadn't been a loyal son and given his family what they demanded— a respectable marriage with a heir— he'd have stayed a bachelor as well. And stayed here."

"You're a loyal friend, Amos." Peter was almost envious of the older man. "Twenty some years is a long time to keep a candle in the window."

"Not when the one you're waiting for is the only one you want." It was said with depth of feeling; Peter believed every word of it. To find love, even a love that couldn't be spoken about, was possible. He had to believe that. "You'll learn that. If you're lucky. Neal is perfectly suited to you. He'll see that right off. Jonathon was to have discussed it all with the lad."

Peter gave a frustrated grunt. While it was not uncommon for two bachelors or widowers who worked together to share living space, and develop a longstanding companionship, no matter which side of the trough they drank from, Peter's quiet life had been in upheaval ever since these two older matchmakers had decided he was the answer to bringing respectable stability and happiness to Neal Clifton's young life, while adding companionship to his own lonely existence. It was frustrating.

And so very appealing.

He hoped Clifton was a tolerable sort, and a little more pleasant to look upon than the balding, barrel-chested senior Clifton was.

Not that he himself was a frail man. Being a silversmith needed more than an artist's eye for fine detail and patience. It required a surprising level of body strength, power and endurance. The average household coffee pot took over two hundred hours of firing, shaping, acid baths and hammering, most of it achieved with the delicate application of sheer brute strength.

At the unusually tall height of six foot one, Peter's sturdy frame was solid muscle, most of it in his thick shoulders and arms set on a sturdy pair of long, strong legs all clothed under shirttails, plain brown waistcoat, leather breeches and thick stockings. His hair was not overly long as was the current gentleman's fashion, but he still preferred it tied back with a strip of brown leather that nearly disappeared against the color of his hair.

The hour chimed on the ornate fireplace clock, a keepsake from his late father, a lethargic winding down of time, a reminder of domestic chores still undone for the day. He sighed and put his latest commissioned piece down on the tall table that served as his client display area.

"Put on your best courting manner, Peter. He'll be here soon. Take it from a man who knows, don't let this chance slip away, my boy." Amos patted him on the back and walked toward the front shop, whistling a tune Peter recognized as something the vicar's wife sometimes sang at church gatherings. Usually weddings.

"Amusing, Amos. Very amusing." Amos merely winked at him and continued without losing a note.

The tune was whipped away on the blustery wind as

the door was suddenly thrust open. A lean, hurried form swept into the room along with the chill blast of air.

Peter started forward as the new arrival shrugged off hat and scarf and turned to face Amos. The sight froze Peter to the spot, feet suddenly stuck to the flooring as if he had gone completely lame. His stomach clenched, his expression instantly melting into a startled look of delight before he could temper it.

The slight, pale skinned man before him was beautiful. A slender, dark-haired angel with watery, startlingly blue eyes, a delicate straight nose bracketed by high cheekbones, and framed by waves of chestnut brown. Of average height, he stood many inches shorter than Peter. Drenched, he couldn't weigh much more than half of Peter's sizable weight.

Peter could see the elder Clifton in the dazzling smile that instantly animated the slender pink lips. There was no doubt in his mind who this young man belonged to, but Neal Clifton obviously had inherited his mother's attributes—slim, delicate featured, almost petite, but undoubtedly male. The late Mrs. Clifton must have been a truly awe-inspiring, magnificent woman to have given birth to such a man considering her husband's plain, rugged looks.

A small ache of desire hit his gut. This beautiful man would never want him. Peter had to work hard to push the burst of longing back into the furthest corner in his heart where he kept such unacceptable thoughts and feelings.

"Good day, Mr. Ro—Amos." The young man smiled shyly and nodded to the older man. The upturned corners of the wind-reddened lips coupled with the honest pleasure at seeing Amos endeared him to Peter immediately. The young man apparently respected and honored his father's friends. "It's unexpected to see you away from your place of business on such a busy day."

Neal's voice was like buttery soft leather, a little breathless from the cold, but medium-pitched, well-mannered, slightly-hesitant, and self-effacing. A touch of humor to it. There was no trace of snobbery or entitlement, as Peter feared the young son of a wealthy man might have.

He was mesmerized by the small Adam's apple just above the notch of Neal's collar. It bobbed up and down as the young man swallowed nervously, blue eyes darting to skate a quick glance across Peter's face again and again as he smiled at Amos. It pleased Peter more than it really should that he made Neal anxious and unsure. A man that looked like Neal Clifton need never be unsure of his welcome in any company.

Amos chuckled, patting Neal's arm, urging him further inside the shop, herding him toward Peter. "Performing a merciful act, son. Delivered a bit of supper for the two of you so you aren't subjected to this man's cooking come evening."

Peter shot Amos a dark look which the man heartily ignored.

"You'll be wanting to spend the entire afternoon and evening together discussing business and whatnot. Make use of Peter's guest chamber for the night if need be." It was more of a command than a suggestion, one that left both Neal and Peter staring wordless at the other. Neal was the first to recover.

"That's very...kind of you, Amos. But I have yet to even make Mr. Wade's acquaintance let alone impose on his hospitality." Neal acknowledged Peter with an embarrassed glance and tentative smile. "Would you do me the honor of a proper introduction, sir?"

"My pleasure, lad. Couldn't think of anything I'd like to do more." Amos grinned that wide smile that seemed to swallow his face and motioned Peter forward. This time Peter found his feet actually responded to his silent command to move. "Mr. Peter Wade, may I introduce to you your new business partner, Master Neal Clifton."

"I believe you are expecting me, sir." Neal hesitated, hand extended.

"A pleasure. And I do mean that. Your father praised your business sense and talent but failed to mention you were a man of handsome stock."

He casually wiped his hands against his breeches to remove the sweaty sheen that had suddenly appeared on his palms. Despite his best efforts, he noticed a tremor as he gripped Neal's hand. "At your service, Mr. Clifton."

"You flatter me, sir but if I may be bold, please, call me Neal."

The smaller hand slipped into his, warm, smooth and fine boned. He gripped it firmly to hide his own slight shuddering movement and found strength in the slender fingers as well. Strength, charm *and* beauty?

This was going to be a difficult day.

Desire rippled up Peter's arm. It ran down his spine like hot silver poured into a sand mold, beautiful and dangerous. His cock stirred, filling with each pulsing beat of his wildly pounding heart, trapped and hidden by leather breeches.

"Not 'sir'. Peter." He stared down into wide eyes so gleaming wet they were tiny oceans. "If you'll pardon the intimacy of it."

A *very* difficult day.

"Yes, please. I'd be delighted to become more intim—" Peter found the faint blush that tinged the high cheekbones endearing. And intriguing. "More familiar…I mean, it's only appropriate since I have requested you call me by my Christian name." Neal glanced around the shop at the commissioned wares, flitting gaze pulled back to Peter's face time and again, then moving off.

A flirting gesture? Does he know of his father's more personal plans?

Long dark lashes feathered against smooth, clear skin. A thin slice of tongue, pink and wet, darted out to simply touch an upper lip, seductive in its innocence. Peter sighed soundless.

An *impossible* day.

Unthinking past the thrill of Neal's warm, firm touch, Peter raised his free hand and clasped Neal's wrist, effectively trapping the younger man in his grasp. Time slowed, savoring the moment, then Neal eased away, his radiant smile overshadowed by uncertainty. Peter was sure he'd over step his bounds.

Two minutes in the man's company and Peter felt completely exposed, vulnerable. He was allowing himself to be seduced by physical beauty without knowing the man underneath. Maybe Neal wasn't as attracted to him as Peter was to Neal. His hands, still wanting to hold on to Neal, now found little comfort tightly gripping the front edge of his waistcoat.

"Had a traveler stop by the inn this morn, brought news from Boston." Amos casually slipped into the growing silence in the room. "Seems a judge there was found dead. Judge Martin Williams. You might have heard his name."

"Yes, I knew of the Judge. A prominent man."

"He was known to many, even outside of Boston. And feared by most who knew him well. Had a fondness for heathen cultures and black arts. Even kept a voodoo princess as a servant from one of his trips to the black islands. Can't say I'm surprised he's met with a sudden end to his days."

Neal's stomach dropped to his toes. He tried not to let his expression change but the vision of Williams laying on the floor of his bed chamber, ghastly gray and cold, was too much. He felt the blood drain from his face. He couldn't keep his gaze from darting to the darkened corners of the room to check for any signs of the insidious cloud of swirling gray. Coughing lightly Neal used his handkerchief to cover his trembling lips.

"A natural death, Amos?" Peter moved closer, his towering frame and substantial girth solid and reassuring to Neal. He felt the wash of paralyzing fear fade to a tolerable level, his heart still pounding against his ribs but not painfully so.

"Didn't say." Amos pulled his hat on and buttoned his jacket, preparing to leave. "Found him in his bed chamber. Not a mark on him. Some business about a broken desk drawer and a rumor about a man skulking about but there weren't much but gossip at this point. Your father might bring more reliable news when he arrives."

He grabbed the shop's door handle and paused a grim, thoughtful expression tightening his wide mouth into a pursed scowl. "Not that it matters. Not to speak ill of the dead, but the world's a better place for it if you ask me." Amos yanked open the door and ducked his head into the wind. He was gone with barely a nod in their direction. A plain spoken man of action.

An uncertain silence settled around them in the void Amos' leaving created. Neal brought his gaze back to study Peter, then shifted to the man's empty hands. "For such... sizable hands, your work possesses a distinctive grace and skill. I can see why father chose you." He forced his gaze away from Peter's large, graceful hands—and the things Neal's imagination wanted them to do to him. "To...to join our strengths."

Strong hands, ones that used their strength to create beauty not pain.

He remembered every harsh touch and painful grab Williams had inflicted on him. The weight in his jacket pocket seemed to grow heavier. Neal slipped his hand into his pocket to reassure himself all was normal, but jerked back out almost as quickly as he had inserted it, the metal so cold it felt like fire.

Was it the wind gusting under the threshold or did he actually hear a moan whisper past his cheek? Guilt and shame squeezed his chest but a glance at Peter's solid, reassuring presence melted the spasm as if it was never there. Neal felt his face heat and hoped it wasn't too noticeable, though he didn't know how anything could escape the other man's intense, searching stare.

These large hands were different; he could tell by the way Peter had cradled his, fingers supporting his wrist, warming his winter-chilled skin, a firm handshake, but nothing more. No crushing squeeze to show dominance. Just restrained, careful strength. A flash of desire hit. Was there such a thing as a powerful man who was gentle?

Somewhere from a dark corner in the room Neal imagined he heard a soft moan or whisper. He tried to ignore it, but a flicker of white off to one side send a chill down his spine even when he realized it was a wisp of smoke from the hearth. The fire snapped and he nearly jumped, covering the move with brisk rub of his hands as if they were still cold. Which indeed they were, his whole body was numb with a cold that had little to do with the weather.

"I—" Something very personal flickered in the steady stare. Peter's eyes were dark brown as the graphite and clay crucibles used to melt silver and gold. "Your workmanship. They're…" he couldn't resist the pull of the man's hands, "…impressive." Everything about this man was.

Peter Wade was handsome in a rugged, daring fashion that brought visions of the heroes in the stories his mother told him as a child. A towering man, Peter was broad in shoulders with hearty upper arms that sprouted from a muscular chest undoubtedly honed by many hours swing a malling hammer. This man labored hard at his craft.

"While I have learned my father's trade well and enjoy it, I lack the power and endurance that you and he share by virtue of your stalwart bodies."

Peter's gaze measured Neal from head to toe. A small smile tugged the man's firmly held lips into motion. "I've seen your work as well. And *your* appearance suits *you*, sir. Your work possesses a grace and delicate skill. It is obvious to me now where that comes from."

Peter paused, his focus moving off into the darker corners of the room before looking back at Neal, a new daring light in his eyes as if he had made a decision. His shoulders straightened marginally. It seemed to Neal he took on a more confident, assertive air out of whatever thoughts had struck him.

"The day grows long and I have yet to sit down to a warm meal. It would be a shame to let Amos' generosity got to waste by having it go cold. Would you join me? My living quarters are in the back. We'll sit by the fire and chase off that chill wind that followed you into the shop."

Peter shuttered the shop window and locked the door to show he was closed then moved down the hallway, one large, firm hand guiding Neal with a small push on his lower back. The hand stayed there as they walked, its solid presence calming the rippling terror running down his spine. It felt possessive and intimate and...right.

If only the whispering voice would stop! Even Peter's rich timber of speech couldn't completely block it out.

"One of the schoolmaster's daughters tidies up for me and stocks the cupboard a bit, but not more than bread and cheese. A real meal will be an appreciated change. Amos is a thoughtful friend to share his cook's wares. Come."

Wordlessly, Neal hurried along, hoping to leave the disembodied whispering behind.

Down a narrow hallway they entered the tidy back kitchen, a fire dying low, Amos' supper pot warming near the embers. Off to one side a half open door revealed a bedroom, but Neal could see nothing more than a thick rug and a tall dresser as they passed by.

A shake of the grate, and the addition of coal under Peter's expert hands, and the fire crackled to a comforting blaze. The gusting wind whistled down the chimney blessedly silencing the moan that had followed Neal, caressing his cheek like a feathery touch of icy fingers.

The sudden absence of the chilling sound made Neal weak in the knees. Loss of sleep and little food these last few days didn't help. He stumbled, bracing for the fall, fervently hoping he could blame his unsteadiness on the dim light and unfamiliar surroundings.

An arm wrapped around his waist like an iron band to hold him upright, his fall transformed into a slight stumble. He looked up and was captured by Peter's steady gaze only inches from his own. The man's eyes were three different colors of brown; all jagged edges packed together, bright and shining clear, like tiny stained glass windows. He smelled of leather and body heat, tinged with a faint musky scent Neal recognized as arousal. He just couldn't be sure if it was Peter's or his own. He was back on his feet with nothing more between them than a breathless look. Peter's arm disappeared, but a hand gripped his shoulder.

"Your father mentioned I was a life-long bachelor?" It wasn't what he expected Peter to say but it broke the awkward moment.

"He did share that he thought your life somewhat lacking in companionship." Neal searched Peter's face for some reaction to his words. "Of...any kind."

"Life has taught me to be a man of few wants or needs. And those that I do have I've learned to keep to myself." A curt, automatic reply that had an undercurrent of emotion Neal could feel all the way to the bright buckles on his shoes.

Pausing briefly in his step, Peter added in a thoughtful, vaguely frustrated tone, "Your introduction to my life looks to change that, I'll wager."

§ § §

They talked over business and politics, silver molds to favored hammering techniques. Neal asked about the best blacksmith to the most able cobbler in town.

The conversation started out stilted but Neal's natural exuberance took hold. He gradually coaxed out more from the other man than Peter's quiet, short comments. They relaxed into the pleasure of the other's company.

Despite their outward differences, they discovered they had many things in common. During a rare silence between them, Neal caught the other studying him—his movements, his clothing, his face—an intent, openly appraising look about him. Neal felt he saw approval in the measured glance. That thought shot a thrill to his loins.

"I must give your father his due, Neal. He is a shrewd man. In his business sense and his assessment of human nature." It was said slowly as if Peter was talking to himself, remembering little things he once disregarded as unimportant. "He foretold that we would be... companionable."

"That we do seem to be, sir. I am ease with you like I have been with no other so quickly."

"He cautioned me that you would be my balance—'a graceful sweep of charm and whimsy to compliment my...more sturdy design'." His smile widened, showing Neal just how handsome he was.

Neal had to stop himself from leaning toward the man, a twenty-year-old's willpower wavering in his mere days-old resolve to ignore his body's physical desires.

"Was he evaluating our craftsmanship or our character?" Neal needed time to sort out the attraction he was feeling—a mutual attraction he hoped.

He was surprised when Peter purposely leaned in close to him. "I believe he may have been clever enough to be referring to both."

Neal smiled brightly, excited by the man's closeness but afraid of misreading Peter's intent. "My father is an intuitive man, maybe more so than I had suspected."

Peter laughed but didn't pull back. "He was right about you. Your presence inspires me to bring more beauty to my life." There was that appreciative glint again, along with a roguish smile.

"You flatter me, sir." He couldn't help the self-conscious smile. It felt good to be treated with kindness and respect. Neal would have blushed if another man had said that, but Peter appeared at ease with making a brash, flirtatious compliment.

This bold attitude intrigued Neal. And scared him. He knew what it was to be drawn in by a charming, assertive man.

The accursed pocket watch weighed heavily in his waistcoat pocket, cold and stark, reminding him of why this wasn't a wise course of action. Which was the reason he had kept it, wasn't it? His conscience in a twisted gold box. One he would gladly dispense with right now.

And just like that, Williams invaded his thoughts, the ghostly specter of guilt. He shoved the memory away and thought instead of Ayana. He'd heard no word on ruling of the judge's death yet but he feared for the woman. He hoped the letter he had left with the stable boy for his father would provide her aid if it was needed. Ayana had never really seemed to need or want anyone. For any reason.

Unlike the way Neal now wanted the man before him. That undisguised glint in those steady brown eyes was surely desire. Neal had seen it in many a man's eye before but he only had the courage, disastrous as that turned out to be, to return the interest once.

Until now. A shiver teased his spine but he wasn't sure if it was excitement or fear.

Undeniably, caution was needed. He had to be sure. He couldn't afford another mistake of the heart. Why was he cursed with these nagging needs and desires of the flesh? But then Peter appealed to him on more than a physical level. In the short time they had known each other he had found a sense of safe haven no other had given him.

"I have heard great praise for Wade House and its proprietor. High praise." Neal's furtive gaze wandered over Peter's towering frame, lingered on the fit, firm torso and well-defined musculature to end at the man's rugged face. Peter's lips, parted in a soft smile, coupled with the unmistakable heat in his stare, grabbed Neal's gaze and held it tight. Desire hit him hard in the gut forcing out fervent, heated words before he could stop them. "And justly so, sir."

With near-panicked effort, Neal tore his gaze away. He needed time to think and he couldn't keep looking into Peter's bold eyes.

His father had nothing but praise--*continual* praise, now that Neal thought about it, for Peter Wade and Wade House. Hard working, respectable bachelor, successful, devoted to his craft, a stout loner with a fine heart and an artist's soul. Neal could see it all in the man before him. That and more. He could see sensual power and gentle hands, soft gazes and bold confidence. Strength and desire, passion and want.

A coldness burned his thigh, a circular pain the size of a watch. Neal shifted, opening his jacket so the pocket fell away from his body. It did nothing to slow the sudden pounding of his heart, the dryness of want in his mouth.

Williams had been a 'respectable' man, too, though the elder Clifton had been outspoken with his dislike of the judge. Neal should have listened to his father opinion on his choice of...*company*. Maybe, it was time he listened now.

Peter pulled the pot off the fire. He set the supper and two bowls on the small table. Mugs followed with a healthy measure of wine in each. The carved wood of the table was graceful but sturdy, meant for service not looks yet still pleasing to the eye. Just like the shop and the cozy back living space. A lot like Peter.

"We'll share supper then I'll walk you back to your rooms when you take your leave. There are streets you should avoid at night. Come, sit with me, Neal."

Neal nodded and moved to sit with his back to the fire but Peter gestured at the chair beside him. "No, no. Sit here, facing the hearth. I'm enjoying the way the firelight strikes your face."

It was overly bold. Inexcusable. Neal should object at the impudence and liberty Peter took with the flirtatious comment. He should reject the offered seat, leave the shop and find his own way back to the inn. Any man would. Any man not attracted to other men.

Nervous, excited, wary and pleased, Neal moved to round the table and squeeze past Peter toward the other chair. He was suddenly uncertain when Peter didn't do the gentlemanly thing and step back to widen his passage through the small space. If anything, the man leaned in, purposely brushing their bodies, face to face, gazes latched on to each other. Neal knew his own stare was as nervous as Peter's was daring.

Peter's breath, warm and alive, washed over Neal's lips. Neal wanted to devour the heat, taste the mouth so tantalizingly near, feel the strength and passion he was sure lay under Peter's calm exterior. It hurt to have Peter so near, to drink in the confusing, delightful, terrifying emotions this plain-spoken man instilled in him in such a short period of time. Neal flushed with hesitation, wanting but knowing he should resist, he should hide away until this business with Williams was over.

The decision was taken from him when Peter slowly slid a hand into Neal's unbound hair and pulled him in. Angling Neal's face with a gentle tug of hair, Peter drew closer. He stared into Neal's pleading eyes, his gaze searching.

"I...I..." Whatever Neal was going to say died on his lips. The fireplace clock ticked off two loud, seemingly endless seconds while Peter gave Neal a last chance to say more.

Neal couldn't utter another sound, breathless with the desire to know the touch and taste of the man who handled him with such gentle power and respect.

Then, as if Neal was made of the most delicate silver filigree, Peter closed the distance between their parted mouths and kissed him. It started out as a slow caress of lips, an exchange of panted breath, a gentleman's introduction. The moment their lips parted, heat, moisture and undeniable want mingled on their tongues. The kiss turned wanton, teeth clicking, tongues licking.

Neal wanted to be swallowed down whole, consumed, to become a literal part of the other man, to chase away the whispers, the chill in his bones, the fear that lingered in his heart. His fists twisted in Peter's shirt, the fever of the man's body seeping deep into Neal's skin, connecting them as if they had been molten silver fused together.

Neal could feel Peter's hardness against his side, thick and hot, curved to his hip as if it fit like a missing part of his body. He ground into the heaviness, letting his tongue stroke Peter's palette and tongue in the same rhythm. He yearned to untwist his fingers from Peter's shirt and seek out the other man's cock, to slide it, naked over his palm, to rub its length with his eager shaft until they found release. But just as he began to loosen his grip, Peter ended the kiss, peppering Neal's mouth with soft caresses, gently pulling Neal's reluctant lips away.

"Peter." The sigh escaped with the last wet slip of lip over lip. It sounded broken and hopeful even over the buzz of pounding blood in Neal's ears. Peter's hand tightened in his hair before releasing him and pushing Neal to an arm's length away. An immediate chill invaded Neal, gooseflesh raising on his arms and neck. Confusion battled with the desire to regain his grip on Peter and pulled him back for another embrace. Peter's concerned expression stilled his impulsiveness.

Peter's palm touched Neal's cheek as it withdrew. "I'd offer apology for what would seem at any other time a vulgar taking of liberties, sir, but I don't think I have misunderstood your father's suggestive assurances. Or the look in your eyes."

"What do you see, Peter?" His gaze was so passionate Neal felt as if it raked over his skin like the sharp tines of a fork. A fresh shower of gooseflesh paraded down his spine. He could not trust his limbs to function.

"My own hunger looks back at me, good sir. Hunger and a rare, superb, unequaled, manly beauty. Now that I have known you, though the time has been mere hours, I would forsake all I have in life to call you mine." Peter paused, his jaw squared, his shoulders straight, obviously resigned to accept rejection if it came. But his raw, pleading voice betrayed him. "Tell me I have not laid my soul bare to you only to have it thrown in the dust."

Pressing a hand to Peter's chest, Neal waited for the speed of his racing heartbeat to slacken. He needed the roar in his head to fade. Reason returned with the ebb of blood. "Relieve yourself of any fear of vulgarity or imprudence to me or my honor. I take no offense at your actions or intentions, Peter. Even if considered a perversion of nature to our kinsmen, we are of a like mind and like bodily desire."

He fidgeted and stepped back. Distance. Neal needed time. So much was left unfinished in his old life, the life he was literally fleeing from. Death and madness did not mix with affairs of the heart or loins. He had no right to drag

Peter into his nightmarish madness. The total silence in room was frightening. Not even the ticking of the clock or the hiss of dying flames broke the sudden stillness. "But I must implore of you. I have traveled much this week and find myself in need of more rest than usual. If you will not take offense at the abruptness, I beg you to let me take my leave. I don't wish to stay too late and find the inn barred for the night."

"Surely, the hour is not that late." Peter glared at the mantle clock. "Hell, it's stopped again. The girl that tends to things for me forgets to do it at least twice a week." He moved to the mantle, opened the clock face and affixed the key, turning the gears several times before gracing Neal with a half-amused glance. "Would you care to guess at the proper time? I've lost track for some reason, sweet lips."

It sounded right coming off Peter's lips, a pet name spoken with a comfortable roughness that sent a chill up Neal's spine. But it was the appreciative, lingering gaze that truly distracted Neal. Before he realized what he was doing he had the pocket watch out and its cover released.

His gaze flashed to the pocket watch face, drawn by a sudden sense of cold terror. The creamy white background was gone, occluded by a smoky vapor so dark not even the crisp black hands could be seen. The case vibrated, the audible *tick-tock* of passing time like a disembodied heartbeat pulsing against his sweating, shaking palm.

This couldn't be happening now! Not here, not in front of anyone, but especially not in front of Peter. So far there had been no witnesses to his bouts of madness. He had prayed it would stay that way until he could reach

Ayana to find some answers. The watch burned his hand.

He couldn't bear the sound of the ticking. It gathered strength with each passing second until it thundered in his head. With a cry of pain, Neal threw up his hands to cover his ears, knowing full well he was the only one who heard its accusing beat, but still needing to find refuge from it.

The watch tumbled from his fingers. Gray-black shadows coiled up from the edges of the bent metal, billowing high, gaining length and breath as it rose before Neal's terror-widened eyes. Then suddenly, another movement by the hearth managed to pull his attention away from the horrible, untimely mental aberration.

Peter, expression alarmed, powerful body poised in a defensive stance against the mad man in his home, was all Neal saw before he blocked everything out with a tight squeeze of his eyelids. He would lose everything now. This madness was his undoing. His future was gone and all possible happiness with it.

Willfully blind, he still saw Peter in the blackness behind his closed lids, shocked, confused and ready to physically defend himself.

And the only other thing in the room with Peter was Neal.

This was not good.

Neal was desperate to make Peter understand, but the words wouldn't come. He opened his eyes and stepped toward Peter but the shadows, now a huge, almost opaque mass, opened a black hole like a mouth and wailed its ghastly sound, swirling menacingly between them.

It lunged at Neal.

He fell to his knees nearly weeping, helpless, his shame and guilt exposed and at the mercy of his own dark secret. These were the fruits of his unnatural desires. Neal wanted to curl up and die.

"Neal!"

Peter's voice was strong, concerned but unruffled considering the scene Neal was creating, cowering on the floor, fighting off some specter only he could see.

"Neal, what's happening? What is it?"

"Do not fear me, Peter! Please!" He cringed and ducked as he imagined the shadow striking out at him. "It is but my guilty conscience haunting me, driving me mad."

"The devil that!" It was bold, harsh, forcefully uttered, but not *at* Neal. Neal raised his head to find Peter looking directly at the black specter hovering over Neal's head. "I'm not blind, man! If this is your madness, it afflicts me as well. I see this unnatural shadow."

The room shuddered, another wail bouncing off the plastered walls and bare wood ceiling. Peter seemed to read Neal as if he had known him all his life and understood him at a mere glance. "Here. With us. In this room, Neal. You are not mad. *I* see it. *I* hear its unearthly tongue."

"I'm not imagining it? Truly?" Neal had convinced himself this was all his mind playing tricks, punishment for his own wickedness. It would take more than a moment to dispel the idea, even with Peter's confident insistence.

The gaping mouth stretched wider, the garbled screech wretchedly gruesome. It swayed above Neal then plunged downward, looking for all the world as if it meant to consume him. Neal fell to the floor, a swiping sound slicing the air above him, solid and real. Very solid and real, very unlike the formless mist. He rolled onto his back searching the room for a weapon to fend off his attacker and found Peter had already raced to his defense.

The slicing cut the air again and again, the fireplace poker whipping through the black misty form, powerful, sweeping blows welded by Peter's straining arm. The mist billowed out in trailing clouds of darkness, each blow followed by a bellowed wail of anger.

But that was all the protective blows managed to produce. The ghost was unstoppable.

It dove past Peter, descending straight down on Neal, pinning him on the floor. Its obvious objective was now apparent to Neal, the need to invade Neal's body at any cost. That had been the goal of every attack so far and this one wasn't any different.

"Neal! Neal, *move*!" The air near Neal's head swirled by, the power of Peter's swings singing through the gray cloud.

Body heat touched his skin, intense beside the chill ribbons of cold that still grabbed at his flesh. Peter pushed Neal closer to the floor, trying to insinuate his body between Neal and his attacker. The force of Peter's protective move jarred the watch from Neal's numb fingers. It landed with a thud, the lid snapping shut with a sound as crisp as brittle bone shattering, the rim of the cover staring back at Neal like an empty eye socket.

Long, gray claws tore at Neal's face, prying at his lips then attempting to slither under his hands as he fought to seal off his mouth and nose. When the need for air became too much, Neal instinctively tore at the collar of his shirt, battling to keep the cold, gritty mist from touching his skin.

Suddenly his grasping fingers rubbed over the thin ribbon of the amulet. Ayana's smooth, dark, knowing face swam before Neal's blurred vision. Inexplicably he knew how to fend off the unnatural creature.

Dragging the amulet out from under his shirt he clamped it to his face, holding it over his mouth. The smell of decaying earth and heavy spices was nauseating but the effect was instantaneous.

The ghost rose in the air. Screeches of anger and frustration rattled the window in its pane sending vibrations of terror deep into Neal's bones. The mist seemed to pale to a murky gray, twisted like a spinning child's toy and flew at Peter.

The room spun, Peter's substantial weight suddenly on him then under him. Breath whooshed from his lungs. He was light-headed with the movement, amulet falling away from his face to hang about his neck, the thick scent of earthy spice clinging to his nostril. Cold needles dug at his back. Holding Neal in a fierce bear hug, Peter rolled under the kitchen table.

Gray mist darted at them from every side until Peter reared up, flipping the table on its side, the top facing out, their backs to a wall.

"Back to hell with you, you evil spirit! Be gone!" On his knees, Peter jabbed at the specter, the heavy fireplace poker still in his hand.

The ghostly apparition turned its gaping mouth and talon-like claws on Peter and fear of losing Peter exploded in Neal's chest. It spurred him into action, an unfamiliar clearness of thought guiding his hand.

"Come here, hold me!" Neal rose to his knees, anxiously grabbing at Peter to drawn him nearer. Peter threw him a look that was part confusion, part elation.

"Now?" Peter made it sound like he would consider it if Neal gave him a good enough reason. That unguarded moment, that one word, sealed their future as far as Neal was concerned. His chest burned and his face flushed and something inside of him smiled. He suddenly knew what love was.

Sparing Peter an affectionate, exasperated growl, Neal pulled Peter to him, repeating the bear hug Peter had used only moments ago. He tugged the ribbon on the amulet up and slipped it over Peter's head, the thin fabric thread binding their necks together, their faces brushing.

"It's the only object that it fears! Trust me, Peter!"

He could feel Peter's heart pounding in his own chest, the heavy thud slower than his own racing beat. The ribbon was tight around two necks instead of one, the least little move pulling them closer. Hot breath flowed across his cheek and down his throat, their chests plastered to each other. A thick thigh wedged between his legs, and Neal could feel the swell of Peter's manhood, rigid and hot, though the layers of their breeches. His own shaft stirred, excited by the nearness of the man.

Risking a hesitant glance into Peter's eyes, Neal's gut clenched and a tingling sensation skittered up his spine. Soft brown eyes gazed down at him, questions in the concerned wrinkles around them, but he could see no harshness in the look.

How could a man go through this and not condemn the one responsible was beyond Neal, but it would have to wait until later to be sorted out.

Neal twisted the thread around so the amulet touched both of their lips, their rapid, warm breath releasing the pungent smell of earth, decay and exotic land into the air around them. Peter baulked slightly at having the tattered bag so near but gave in at one pleading look from Neal.

With a final ghostly wail, the pale graying mist swiped at the air with its viciously hooked tendrils then retreated back to the watch, slipping in under the bent lip of the cover.

Quicker than Neal would have thought possible, Peter yanked the ribbon from their necks and dove at the timepiece. He wrapped the amulet strings around the watch tying the lid tightly shut.

An eerie stillness filled the room broken only by the raspy sound of their labored breathing.

§§§

The bound timepiece quivered in the dust on the

floorboards, but no ghastly shadows or gaping mouth tormented them. A faint moan bounced off the kitchen walls but Neal wasn't certain it wasn't the wind in the chimney. A rain storm has rolled in, the soft patter of falling droplets like angel's tears on the roof.

"Tell me."

Emotions rolled across Peter's face. Horror, disbelief, panic, anger, maybe even grief, a split second devoted to each then the next outrageous realization seemed to strike.

Neal wasn't sure which of them made Peter abruptly drag him close, upper arms locked in the man's fearsomely strong grip, lips near his but nothing like passion or heat in Peter's steady gaze. His voice was eerily low and calm for a man who had just battled a demon.

Battled and *won*. Defeated the specter, at least temporarily. Chased it back to its unholy berth in the accursed watch and bound it there. At great possible injury to life and limb. Peter hadn't run, hadn't been rendered helpless or struck dumbfounded by the unnatural events.

He also wasn't speechless.

"Tell me, Neal." Peter punctuated Neal's name with a shake, making him listen. The grip on his arms tightened and then eased slightly. "An ungodly demon seeks to take you from me."

Supportive now instead of restraining, that's how Peter's hold felt. He let the other man take some of his weight, exhaustion, relief, hope, draining away his strength. "You braved a specter of death. Without knowing what creature had come upon us, you fought to protect me. You didn't think me mad!" Neal slumped. Peter lowered him to the floor, back to the wall, then took a place beside him, knees touching, one heavy, comforting hand still grasping Neal's arm.

"I don't think you suffer madness now." He pressed Neal's shoulder back, gently forcing him to raise his bowed head to look Peter in the eye. "Tell me what beast treads along your steps, Neal. For it is my path, at present, as well."

"I have been cursed." Neal choked on the words. Guilt rose up to constrict his throat. He felt lightheaded, nauseous that Peter should hear the facts of his past indiscretions. "Maybe not unjustly, but harshly. Stalked by the evil that sought to possess me when it...he was alive."

"And into death?"

The watch shook, metal and cloth against wooden planks, a rattle like the tiny bird bones Ayana kept in a metal lined box. The wind had turned to a whistle in the chimney, the patter of the rain mimicking distance horses hooves in the dirt. All of the sounds more welcome than the one Neal knew was inside the timepiece.

"Yes. You have the right to the truth after what has just occurred." Neal closed his eyes. There was no other way. Humiliating as it was. "Judge Williams believed in a heathen practice, like an ancient religion of sorts. One he learned during his travels in the Caribbean. It has rituals his servant Ayana still practices. She professes to communicate with the spirits of the dead. He used these same rituals to keep her a prisoner. And now he—his evil spirit—uses it to...*pursue* me."

"Even in death he seeks to possess you?"

"As you have just witnessed. Since...knowing him..." Neal searched Peter's face, hoping not to see disgust or condemnation with his next words, "*knowing* him—" Neal broke off his gaze, then looked back up at Peter, his wide stare pleading. "I would say it was an affair of the heart, but I learned far too late that affection had nothing to do with his desire for me. It was a carnal relationship, nothing more. A perversion such as society sees it."

Peter's hand still lay heavy on Neal's shoulder, steadfast and strong. It gave Neal the courage to reach up and cover the man's fingers with his own. It heartened Neal when Peter didn't object.

"I thought to learn how a man loves another man from a caring soul." Nausea rippled through him again. "I was naïve and foolish. I have no excuse but my inexperience in the ways of the world. Williams desired nothing more than a plaything to manipulate."

Bile burned the back of his throat. He had to swallow several times until he was reassured he wouldn't let humiliation win the moment. "At least, I thought that was all he wanted. Until the night he died."

"You were involved in his death?"

"Only as a witness, I swear! Ayana and I." Neal's gaze darted to the mercifully quiet pocket watch before he gave a jerky nod. "In his bed chamber." He realized what vision his impulsive admission might give Peter. "At least, I think so."

"You don't know?"

"I did nothing! I first went to only retrieve letters!" The fire snapped, the flames occasional small fingers of flickering gold, the room's increasing chill sending shivers up his spine and under his scalp. "Ill-advised letters. Written when the affair was new and wondrous." His chin slumped to his chest, exhaustion leeching his lagging energy away. "He threatened to use them to expose me, to paint me as an unscrupulous seducer of older men, to blight my reputation and humiliate my father. I had to prevent reckless ruin to my family name by my own indiscretions!"

"So you resorted to thievery? Violating a judge's home? You didn't think that reckless?" Peter's dry tone and steely glare made Neal feel hopelessly young and foolish.

"N-not entirely." He grimaced. He took a deep breath trying to steady his voice. "I knew where the letters were kept. Granted, I might have damage the desk drawer opening it, but I didn't violate his home!" It fell weak and quaking into the tense air. "Ayana let me in through the kitchen."

"*Helpful* of your Ayana." The frown pulled Peter's lips into a thin line. The resulting wrinkles around his narrowed eyes spoke of disapproval and disappointment. "To aid and abet in your thievery."

Peter apparently had a generous gift for dry wit. Neal felt physically wounded. His cheeks glowed warm despite his chilled skin.

He wanted to wipe away that harsh expression. "They were my letters. It wasn't really thievery. From my point of view."

"No doubt." The frown eased slightly. "Then what happened?"

"He returned earlier than expected. I do not know why. He was paler than usual but still despicable and cruel. But I cared not for his harsh words and ruinous threats. I had the letters back."

Peter sighed, the first encouraging sign that he was relenting, seeing Neal's unmanageable dilemma. "He let you leave with them without protest?"

"Not...exactly." This was harder than he had hoped it would be. "This would be when he died."

"Tell me."

And with that one strictly spoken command, Neal seemed to completely break. Words poured from him without regard to the madness they revealed, parts rattled off in sputtered half-sentences between distraught gasps. The Judge's collapse, his attempts at the heathen rituals while dying, the horrific appearance of the ghostly demon and its unearthly pursuit of Neal, the damning, and damned, watch Neal didn't dare leave out of his care, and the odd magical protective powers of the servant woman Ayana's worn amulet. It was chaos and lunacy, but Peter had a fairly decent idea of what burdens Neal was carrying.

This young man, this beautiful man, was lean of frame and delicate of feature, but he had backbone and nerve if this demonic spirit had been pursuing him for days. Peter's own heart had yet to calm its heavy beating under his ribs.

That frown was back on his face but Peter fought to keep it in check. It was clear Neal was at the end of his rope. His body trembled with the chill dampness of the rain-soaked air, or the frightful assault they had just endured.

Peter rose, gently prying off Neal's desperate grip when the younger man refused to let him take leave. Avoiding the fallen timepiece, he quickly added more fuel to the fire and returned to sit by Neal. This time shoulder to shoulder, backs to the wall, all eyes turned to study the amulet and its tiny gold prisoner.

"I need to find someone who understands the powers of the amulet. Someone like Ayana. Philadelphia is a large and varied a port as Boston. Surely there are some of Ayana's people here, practitioners of her culture, her spirit ways." Neal's face brightened and he began to rise to his feet. "Sailors would know when human cargo arrived. Servants! Slavers! I could visit the taverns by the docks. I could—"

"Sit!" The stern order stilled Neal's actions but Peter's hand pulled him back to the floor. He added a sharp yank to quelling any thoughts of resistance. "My God, do you ever think before you act?"

The cloud of hurt that fell over those dark blue eyes tempered his anger. Neal had been abused enough by others of late. Peter wanted to be the one who made it better. He had to if he ever hoped of a future with this man. "I see impulsiveness is something we'll have to work on. Together."

"You don't think less of me for Williams? For my desires? My...perversion?"

"How can I condemn a man when the same sin lives within my own heart? I cannot look upon your beauty unhindered by society and law, but I hope to live a secret life of perversion, and happily so. If it is with you."

"You are undaunted by all," Neal gestured weakly at the watch, "this?"

"Sometimes you have to fight for the important things in life." Pulling Neal in close, Peter tucked the dark head under his chin and wrapped his arms around Neal's bowed shoulders, delighting in the way Neal relaxed into the embrace. It took less time than he thought before the regular puffs of warm breath on his skin told him Neal was asleep.

§ § §

Peter passed the hours alternately staring at the watch and gazing at Neal as the other man slept. Eventually, the rhythm of the rain against the windows lulled him into a light doze. He woke to sharp, insistent knocking from the front of the shop. He wiped at his eyes before darting a glance at the amulet bound watch. A second glance at the nearby window showed a muddy gray blur. Night still claimed much of the sky.

Tensely curious about by a pre-dawn caller, he slowly wrestled Neal off his chest, rolling his shoulders to eased their stiffness. If what Neal had said last night about Williams' sudden death, it was not unreasonable to suspect the law could be in pursuit of the young man.

Neal mumbled something, his heavy-lidded eyes bloodshot, locks of dark wavy hair tousled against one cheek partially obscuring the lines on his face from being pressed into Peter's shirt. The faint shadow of beard accented the fine angle of his jawline and fairness of his complexion.

"Peter?"

Even disheveled and incoherent—possibly because of it—Peter was struck all the more by Neal's refined attributes. Undeniably, the man delighted Peter's appreciation and love of physical beauty. No one, man or woman, could gaze upon young Clifton and not be taken by his good looks. He also knew Neal to be prosperous, a skilled tradesman from a respected family, but now he knew him to be of good heart and true intentions, if foolishly impulsive at times. The man beside him was more frightened youth than evil seducer or murder. Peter felt that despite what was happening with this bewitched specter, these events were happening *to* Neal, not because of him.

"Peter, what is it?" Neal lurched to his feet, unsteady, back to the wall, gaze flickering from Peter to the amulet and watch. "Who would call here at this hour? Have they come for me?"

"It will be alright." The moment he had vanished the ghost, nay, more likely from their first kiss, Peter had fallen into the role of Neal's protector. It seemed natural and right like the comfortable fit of his favorite smithy tools against his hand.

Whomever was trying to bang their knuckles raw on his door would the first in what he suspected would be a long series of challenges if Neal remained in his life. At least he hoped so.

"I shall see to it. Whomever it is." He pressed his lips to Neal's forehead as he pushed him back into the shadows of the room. "Be silent and still." Neal's frightened, wide-eyed stare and trusting nod pulled at his heart.

The wind rattled the shutters, but the rain had abated. Before crossing to the door, Peter coaxed an ember to life, pulling a flame out to light a candle. Rumpled, a strand of his thick brown hair hung loose from the cord at his neck. He made no effort to dispel the idea he had been asleep. And alone. If constables were on the other side of his threshold, he couldn't afford to let them become too curious or intrusive. Neither Neal nor a moaning watch in the middle of his kitchen floor would be easily explained.

Releasing the bolt, he cracked open the door, holding the candle out to illuminate the caller. A dark cloak, mud-stained and worn, was draped tightly around a small figure. Brown hands made of delicate bones and callus skin held the fabric close against the grasping wind.

Relieved this was no constable, Peter open the door wider, but remained wary. This was no hour for casual callers.

"Wade House does not open until morning, madame."

"I have not come to buy pretty things, Master Wade."

"Then why pull me from my bed, mistress? Who be you?"

"A servant, sir. I bring news to Master Clifton from his father." Her voice was soft but firm, rich with exotic tone, words oddly clipped, almost musical. Unfamiliar with the accent, Peter found himself straining to understand her.

"Clifton lodges at the Ram's Head." Wind caught the hem of the cloak's hood and pulled it back. Her caramel skin was smooth over broad cheekbones and an oval face. Cat-shaped, wary eyes as black as ink studied him. He felt their penetrating stare drag over every inch of his skin like ghostly fingertips. He absently shrugged his shoulders to shake off a sudden chill. "Seek him there."

A bold gust of air swiped at the candle. It carried the sharp scent of spice and earth to Peter, triggering a mild feeling of unnamed panic. The flame flickered and almost extinguished. Peter hurriedly drew back to shut the door. Woman or not, she affected him oddly. He couldn't be sure she wasn't some extension of the unnatural forces pursuing Neal.

"Please! I beg of you. For both your sakes. Tell him Ayana has come to help." Her pale brown lips tensed in a pursed line. Her fingers gripped the cloak more tightly.

"Ayana?" Peter's head cocked to one side, recognition instantly hitting him. Suspicion ebbed but he was still wary. According to Neal, this woman was much more than an ordinary servant and had played a key role in Neal's present deadly dilemma. "*Neal's* Ayana?"

"Aye, sir. The foolish child's Ayana." Her small smile was wan but genuine. It brought a light to her dark eyes that softened the foreign, black depths. As difficult as it was to judge her age her tone was very maternal toward Neal. "Truer words than you may think, Peter Wade."

"I don't understand your meaning, Ayana, but then I haven't understood much of the last day." Peter swung the door wider and urged her into the room with an impatient gesture. "Swiftly, please. Neal will be relieved to see you safe." He bolted the door.

Towering over her, one hand on her back, Peter guided her toward the back of the shop. Her plain skirt rustled softly, boots tapping on the floorboards in her haste. Ayana dropped her cloak on a chair as she passed it, attention focused in the direction Peter had pointed. He followed close behind.

"Child? Show Ayana your gentle face, boy. Show me I am not too late." Quick, sure steps crossed the small kitchen, unerringly headed toward the shadowed corner of the room where Neal secreted himself.

A muffled, low shriek rattled near her feet, the bound watch quivering against the wooden floor. She stopped cold, eyes wide in fear at the discovery of the evil trinket so close. The wail died away, but Peter felt the air was suddenly thick, heavy with natural tension.

"Ayana?" Neal hesitantly stepped out of the darkness. "Are you truly here? I've prayed to see you every night since this nightmare began." Groggy, blurry eyed, he hurried to meet her but stumbled.

Peter was at his side, righting him, supporting him until he regained his balance. Neal gave him a grateful smile that Peter returned along with a roughly murmured,

"*Our* nightmare. You won't be abandoned to manage this on your own, Neal."

"I have come to help destroy this evil, child." Ayana edged around the watch. Once she was at Neal's side she touched his cheek. "You will need my help to overcome this darkness from the grave."

Peter was struck by the dramatic contrast between her rich brown skin on Neal's pale, fair face. This whole event, weeks of trials and horrifying confrontation had pushed the younger man near his limits.

Only slightly self-conscious, he squeezed Neal's shoulder, pulling him closer to his side. If this woman knew of Neal's real relationship with Williams, she knew his heart. Peter wasn't going to betray Neal by hiding his own feelings around Neal's most trusted confidants. Men cut from the cloth that he and Neal were could not let pride nor fear extinguish true feelings in their hearts.

Pressing her hand to his face with his own shaking finger, Neal let the guilt he had been carrying turn his voice into a raspy, anguished whisper. "I thought you might have been blamed for Williams' death. I should have stayed with you to face them."

"No, you were right to go. I forced you to go. It was much easier to explain events without you being present."

Peter wasn't certain what was happening but he knew he needed to stand back and let Ayana put some of Neal's constant fears to rest. Only she could fill in the blanks of these last few critical days for them both. It was her amulet binding the spirit inside the watch, her rituals that might free them. Peter's and Neal's entire future depended on this woman.

"I'm so sorry I left you there to handle the whole thing. It was cowardly of me." Neal's voice broken slightly, the dim candlelight glimmering wetly in his vibrant eyes.

"Hush, child. You did what was best for both of us. You father received your letter, child. He handled everything. He obtained my legal freedom after the Judge's passing and all accepted the death as weakness of the heart."

"What about the broken drawer?"

"They said it was his own doing looking for the powders his doctor had prescribed for him."

"Doctor?"

"The Judge's frequent 'indigestion'. No one knew but his doctor." Sheepishly, she gave Neal an affectionate smile. "In the end, the Judge had few friends to question his passing."

"And, sir," she bowed slightly, as much teasing as respectful a gesture. "I serve the Clifton household. Your father has been very generous and kind to me."

"But now," her gaze darted to the bound watch, fearful, dark but determined. Voice low, raw, almost angry, her accent became heavy, difficult for Peter to grasp at times. "I have much to tell you, child. Things you will not understand but must accept."

Peter frowned. "I don't like the sound of this."

Ayana's dire tone and Peter's unhappy reaction unheeded, Neal remained focused on the living villain that had occupied his life for so many months. "The watch. Did anyone note it was missing?"

"No. No one. The men with him that night say the Judge was unsteady, ill, last they saw him. He must have dropped it on the journey home. They think it long gone in the hand of a beggar. No one cared that he passed, Neal. No one."

"I can't believe it." Neal straightened, back still to the wall, but the worry lines that marred his face lessened. "I was so sure constables were at my heels." Neal blew out a long breath then froze. "Williams' neighbor. He saw me that night. Going into the house. Mr. Abbott? He said nothing?"

"Abbott had no affection for the Judge." Ayana's laugh was brittle. "He was appointed to the judge's position with the court. He will keep his own counsel, I think."

"Then it's truly over." He slumped further down the wall, head hanging.

Peter wanted to take him in his arms, bury Neal's worried, pale face on his chest and protective him from the world.

Slowly raising his head, he found Peter's anxious, stern face. "I'm not mad and I'm free, Peter."

The watch shook so hard the rattle echoed off the walls. The wail held a note of rage in it, enough so that Neal jerked upright, one hand grabbing Ayana's offered fingers. The other hand stepped away from it to brace his back on the wall. Peter moved with him, angling his body so he blocked the watch from Neal's line of sight.

"*Almost* free, Neal. Almost. We *will* vanquish this obstacle as well. I swear it. Together."

"We must work quickly. The amulet will only hold the Judge's spirit for so long."

"What does it want?" Peter shook his head. "I know it wants Neal, but what does it want him for?"

"An unimaginable horror. A new body. A new life." She placed her open palm on Neal's chest. It rose and fell, fast and shallow, plain for all to see, measuring every rapid breath Neal took. "He practiced some of the most ancient and dark rituals of my people on you. His dark soul called to it. He was preparing for death. His spirit is eager to possess you, Neal, to have a new home so the Judge can live on. He chose this over the grave that awaits him."

Gloom hung in the air, pushing at the walls of the small kitchen, oppressive as a wool cloak. A chill seeped into his tense muscles, his skin hypersensitive to pressure in the room, his body responding to the anxiety, the instinct to protect mixed with desire. He understood the urge a man would have to make Neal his own. He felt it down to his bones, but unlike Williams, it also touched his heart.

Peter turned away to tend the fire. "I would see him put into that grave before this is done."

"Seducing Neal was all part of his plan. Rituals to baptize him with the signs of the afterlife, mark his young body with his own foul scent so his ghost could find Neal at the right time. He knew he would die soon. The doctor's powders did no good. He cared only for himself.

Always for himself."

"I should have seen it. He treated me like an object, like that watch. Useful only when he wanted. A possession." Neal colored faintly, looking more youthful than his twenty-two years. "The knowledge it was not real love came to me too late. I was lost by then, my honor gone, my heart dead."

"He was an evil man." The pain on Neal's face was cutting. Peter wanted to embrace him but settled for offering verbal comfort.

For now.

"You didn't deserve what he did to you, Neal. The betrayal. The abuse. He didn't—couldn't care for you." Voice rough, needy. Even across the room his desire for the other man was obvious. "Your heart is not dead." He paused to summon his courage. He would prefer to bare his soul in private, but their world was off center, trapped in unnatural events. He feared they didn't have the luxury of waiting. If the spirit should escape again, all might be lost. "At least, I pray 'tis not. I would wish that you would share it with me."

"After all this?" Neal's expression lightened. He straightened, gently moving Ayana aside, and approached Peter. Hesitation, surprise, hope written on his face. "You remain interested in our...partnership?"

Peter glanced toward Ayana. She had drifted back slightly to let the shadows dull her presence, inconspicuous as possible without leaving the room. He shrugged his shoulder, an anxious twitch, letting his reservations slip away with the gesture. "If you will consider one as an equal. Made of both desires of the flesh and of the heart."

Neal flushed, a pink splash of fever on too pale cheeks. "Peter!"

It was merely his name but Peter heard everything he needed to know in it—anticipation, fear, want, desire, embarrassment and—acceptance. He pulled Neal to him, excitement coursing through every limb. It was meant to be a gentleman's embrace, a hearty slap on the back, a manly display of pleasure.

The heat of Neal's lips on his own, the wetness of his tongue, the taste of his mouth was unexpected. He was surprised at the bold move until he realized it was *his* hands entwined in Neal's hair holding his head at the proper angle to kiss, *his* arms drawing the slighter man up to meet chest to chest, *his* strength keeping Neal in place until the man reacted with his own grasping, needy embrace. Breathless and weak-kneed, it was long minutes before Peter loosened his grip. A sharp rattle of metal on wood disturbed the joy.

Spices and earth peppered the air. A blanket of gritty mixture settled over the bound timepiece. The death rattle stopped abruptly. "I know the ritual that will banish this spirit to the darkness once its chosen host is cleansed. I have the needed ingredients with me. I can perform the cleansing ritual here. Now. But I will need help." Ayana rubbed her fingers over her palm to get the last of her potion off her skin and on to the ghost's makeshift, metal lair. "It is good you are prepared to share yourselves."

"What?" Neal ran his hands through his hair, smoothing it back into place from Peter's insistent grasp. He turned to face the woman, the fact he had momentarily forgotten she was still in room written in his flustered movements. "Why?"

"Because it is the only way for you to be rid of this abomination. You must be cleansed of his scent. Obliterated. Replaced." She cast a meaningful, lingering gaze over both men, eyebrow arched, a small smile on her full lips. "By the scent of another, a new *paramour*."

"O-oh."

Undaunted by Neal's embarrassed stutter, Peter stepped up close behind the other man, hand confidently squeezing Neal's shoulder, his voice warm and firm. "I don't foresee that as a problem."

§ § §

Rhythmic chanting, strong, forceful, carried through the closed bed chamber door. Its exotic song, mesmerizing and mystical, darkened the heavy mood of the house. Oppressive as it was, it couldn't dim Neal's anticipation.

Peter built a hurried fire in the hearth to ward off the pervasive chill, then lit a single candle on the bedside table. Its glow flickered dimly, painting the bed with long strokes of gold and gray, the illusion of warmth and comfort, a welcome contrast to what was happening in the shop's small kitchen.

Hurriedly stripping to nothing more than his shirttails, Neal hesitated, idly touching items as he walked to the bed. The chamber was simple but comfortably appointed. The sparse furniture handsome, sturdy, large, like Peter.

The turned back bed was oversized to accommodate Peter's tall height, the matting good quality, thick and firm. The revealed bedding was clean, not the same quality Neal was used to in his father's home, but still cool and smooth under his fingertips. The coverlet's bound edges were ropes of silk, a dark gray wrapped around a massive square of deep blue linen, a shade surprisingly not unlike the color of Neal's eyes. Touches of the same color were used around the room—drapes, chair—obviously a favorite of Peter's.

Sitting on the edge of the bed, he studied Peter's bare back, shoulders long and corded, muscles rippling with every move as the other man crouched, tending the fire. After only knowing each other for a few hours, Peter had stood fast at Neal's side during the ghost's attack, held to the conviction that Neal was not insane, and remained with him through the night. Remained at his side and held him in his arms while he slept, protecting him throughout the night. Peter Wade was a steadfast man, strong, self-confident and unwavering when faced with overwhelming adversity.

Amos liked Peter. His father liked him. Neal liked him. More than liked him. Affection, desire, want, lust, maybe even the start of something more, made his breathing come in rapid puffs, his face warm and his skin tingle. He tore his shirttails over his head and threw them on the bottom of the bed. The damp cold of the room raised gooseflesh all over his body. Despite the cold, other parts of his body responded to the sight of Peter's half-naked flesh. Sliding between the linens, he drew the cover high for warmth and scooted to the center of the huge bed into a position so he could see Peter. And Peter could see him—waiting. Willing. *Wanting.* He let the blankets fall to his lap.

If this had been Williams' chamber he would have had to suffer the Judge's cold, dirty touch and embarrassing insults while the man undressed him. Pain, abuse, shame, remorse would follow rapidly.

None of those things would occur here, except some lingering guilt. He wasn't sure that would ever go away. But he could live with guilt if it meant he could have the possibility of a life and working partnership with this man, secret as the intimacy would have to be all their lives.

Dusting his hands on his breeches, Peter stood from the fire and turned, gaze finding Neal, his expression marked by first surprise and then pleasure. He disrobed as he crossed the few feet to the bed. He was completely naked by the time he reached Neal. It was a bold and confident action. Even married couples rarely completely undressed together, even during intimacy. It unnecessary, shameful, exciting and wanton.

Neal knew what strength it had taken for him to completely undress. He couldn't see any of the hesitancy he had felt in Peter's smooth movements. His smile was just as bold as his actions, his intense, needy gaze devouring Neal's, taking in everything. Neal felt desired, hungered for, as if he was the only thing Peter required to be whole.

Peter climbed onto the bed on all fours, a stalking mountain lion approaching its prey. And just like a frightened deer, Neal froze in place, stare lost in Peter's devouring gaze, waiting for the pounce. Peter wrapped a muscle bound arm around Neal's hips and yanked him closer and down.

He lay flat on his back, arms flung over head in the suddenness and strength of the move. Heat radiated into his side, body heat mingling, warming his chilly skin, a blanket of comforting flesh encasing him on one side. Peter bent over him, looming close, a smile of pleasure on his square, rugged jaw, his lips silent yet parted.

Hard and growing harder, every inch of his body tense, tingling with anticipation and lust, Neal studied Peter's face as it slowly drew nearer. The man was undeniably handsome, brown eyes like the finest burl woods, multi-shades of brown and gold dotted, surrounded a lake of black. Neal liked the way their gaze darted across his own face, followed by Peter's hand, touching his cheek, his hair, his jaw line, his lips, drinking in every part of him, seeing the cut of him, seeing *him*.

Leaning close, Peter slipped one arm under Neal's head, the other curling around his back to pull Neal closer. Agonizingly slowly, Peter touched his lips to Neal's, a soft greeting, gentle and short lived.

A wailing moan, muffled and distant but louder than Neal expected leeched through the closed bedchamber door. The chanting rose for several seconds them lowered as the moan subsided. Neal sighed when Peter broke the kiss.

"Peter?" Did they get this far only to have the man not want him?

Peter lifted his head, barely separating their mouths.

"Are you alright? Do you truly wish this, Neal?"

Words couldn't be found to answer adequately so he didn't try to find them. Wrapping both arms around Peter's neck, he pulled the man down, pressing their bodies together. Hard cock knocked hard cock as their mouths met, teeth clicking, jaws open and devouring. The embrace became heated, insistent, almost frenzied. And it was Neal doing the insisting. Their tongues clashed, Peter's demanding possession of Neal's mouth, giving breath and slick wetness over in exchange for control. His lips tasted faintly of salt, stale from their forced night on the floor but rich, masculine.

Desire pushed aside mundane thoughts, the very core of Neal's being flushed with need and wanton lust. His soul cried out for release from the burden of guilt he had been carrying. The urge for acceptance and rakish carnal pleasure blotting out all else. Even the ghastly events happening outside the bed chamber were as distant as a half forgotten dream.

Groaning as his head was angled back by Peter's large hand, blunt fingernails scratching his scalp as his hair was combed out of his face. Lips peppered slow, soft kisses along his brow and down his cheek, over his jaw line and back up the other side. A thick thigh slid between his legs holding them apart as Peter rocked against Neal's body, stiff cock nudging his sac, teasing his shaft, heat and wetness and silk all at once.

"Lord God!" The sensations were almost too much for Neal to tolerate.

True to his nature, Peter used action instead of words

even in this. The kisses never stopped, light touches to Neal's closed eyelids, a breathy, moist trail down one cheek, then finally reclaiming his mouth, invading and conquering him all over again. When Neal began to toss his head wanting more, Peter began working his way down Neal's neck and chest, claiming very inch of flesh as his own.

Moaning, Neal arched his back, thrusting up into Peter's long torso. His nipples were hard and burning, wanton, like begging things. Peter pressed his thumbs, hard, pushing and rubbing, making Neal groan with pleasure. His hips worked against Peter's hard abdomen, pinned between flesh and linen. He tossed his head to one side, baring his neck, silently begging.

He thrust up again, pressing his chest into Peter's hands, his rough thumbs. Nails pinched lightly then harder. Neal shuddered, his nipples like glowing embers, burning hard, eager. Peter licked at them in turn then sucked one into his mouth and teased it between his teeth. The other nipple felt abandoned until a rough thumb and finger plucked it back to fiery life.

Hips bucking, Neal grasped Peter's shoulders with both hands, using him for leverage to gain more friction. Peter rolled slightly, teeth still latched on Neal's taut nub. Neal gasped at the loss of body heat. He choked back a protest as calloused fingers brought both cocks together and began massaging the stiff lengths, pulling back foreskins to rub the exposed heads.

A sharp nip at his aching nipple shot rivers of fire like the rays of a sunburst across his chest. He pushed up into Peter's lips, a grunt escaping as the nub was flicked by a wet tongue, suction pulling the crinkled flesh into the heat of Peter's devouring mouth. The sensation raced past pleasure to pain then deep, muffled groans of need that rumbled against his ribs took the pain to a place he could only describe as ecstasy. Several short, harsh strokes on his shaft, a swirl of callus around the rim of his swollen cock head, and Neal tipped over the edge.

"Mother of God! Peter!"

Body fluid coated Peter's pumping hand, smoothing the strokes as the other man wrung the last of Neal's joy from him. Peter licked the sweat from Neal's chest, moving up to take his panting mouth in a searing kiss. As the orgasm faded, he realized the kiss had gentled.

Peter shifted his weight, resting between Neal's spread thighs. Neal was still panting, trying to refocus his vision in the dim room as Peter slowly breached his opening with a wet, smooth finger, both large, square hands under Neal's ass, long arms finding Neal's opening with ease.

"Are you with me, Neal?" The finger went deeper, finding Neal's sweet spot, sending bellows of heat through his lower gut, loosening his instinctive resistance, sending reason and the power of speech to some locked corner of his fevered brain. He nodded. Peter kissed him again then rolled to one side, weight still heavy on Neal, one hand kneading the curve of his ass. Peter lifted to one knee, pulled Neal into a better position beneath him. His cock replaced his finger and he slowly began working deeper, a smooth rocking motion, back and forth, patiently joining them.

Steeling himself against the surge of pain he had come

to expect with this, Neal squeezed his eyes shut, fists twisted in the pillow under his head. It took him some time before he realized Peter has stilled and was talking to him, a low soothing murmur, calm but with an underlying thread of strain.

"Neal? Open your eyes. Look at me. Show me you are here, with me. Not with Ayana. Not remembering someone else. Look at me. This is not to be taken lightly."

Eyes open wide, Neal blinked, more to push away his surprise than to adjust to the darkness of the room. The smell of wood, cotton and Peter filled the air. A faint buzzing dulled his hearing, the sound of his own blood rushing in his veins. His cock ached, embarrassingly soft from the threat of coming discomfort, pleasantly sore from the thoroughness of Peter's earlier attention.

His ass clenched, the stretching burn of penetration constant, fresh and sharp, muscles tense waiting. He'd endured this act before, under the ruthless hand of the Judge. He bit back the memory. He would endure anything if it meant being rid of Williams' ghastly haunting. He hoped Peter would be kind afterward. Know some way to make the taking less gut-wrenching but, he was prepared to settle for it being over quickly.

Peter seemed to have other plans. His thumb gently passed over Neal's lips, rubbing over the wet lower one, an intimate, deeply affectionate gesture.

"You already marked me." He slid his palm down Neal's abdomen, the touch sticky, the scent of his own fluids rising up from Peter's hand. "Now if I'm going to mark you as mine, I want to be the man you see when it happens, in your thoughts and with those beautiful eyes. Just me."

Blinking back a sudden wetness that blurred his vision, Neal nodded. He tried to relax against the bedding, taking deep breathes to ease the tightness in his gut. Peter nodded back, then reached out to force one hand under the folds of bedding, returning with a small silver vial. With an ease that told of regular practice, he deftly pulled the top off and set it spinning off into the shadows, the dull thud of metal to carpet marking its journey.

Uncertain, Neal watched Peter work one handed, a drizzle of oily liquid splashing between their lower bodies, coolness running over their cocks as Peter poured it back and forth. Neal wasn't even aware of where the bottle went after the first slippery stroke of Peter's shaft caressed his passage.

The room faded. Peter's steady stare was all he saw, every nerve in his body feeling as if it were swollen, glutted with lust, brimming with sensation. The pain was carried away on the rush of pleasure, the rub and bump of cock head over the spot inside hitting him like lightning strikes. He arched and rocked, seeking more. Distantly he recognized the gasps and groans as his own over a background of Peter's rhythmic panting grunts.

Heavy hands tugged his hair, wiped the wetness from his cheeks, soothed their drying fluids over his fevered flesh, skin alive and tingling as if dotted by sparks of molten silver from the forge.

His own fingers danced over rippling skin, smoothed the valleys of hard muscle, mapped ribs and spine, freely exploring, taking what was being offered, reveling in having found not only a kindred soul, but a good man as well.

Fingers dug into his hips and pulled him further into Peter's embrace. Urged by guiding hands, Neal draped his calves over Peter's shoulders, his cock stiff and curved to point at his belly. All pain cast off, pleasure devoured him. His ass spread wider, his opening stretched so tightly he could feel the bulging rim of cock as it slid out to its head and burrowed back in again, slick, hot, thick. Testicles smacked against his ass, teasing the spread, delicate skin between his cheeks, regular and hard, spanking him like a searing palm.

His nipples crinkled, swollen, taunt, peaked nubs of flesh full of memory of Peter's mouth against them. The sharp tug of teeth, the bright flare of delicious fire that flowed across his chest, racing straight for his cock. His gut was heavy, oddly full like his swollen cock, the knot of desire building larger, tighter until he was sure he couldn't endure more. Then Peter thrust fast and deep, jerky rough strokes, his hands almost crushing Neal in their grip, his lips demanding, hungry, his taste hot, wet, bathing Neal's mouth with Peter's scent just as his cock was burying his essence in the farthest reaches of Neal's body.

Despite all the care Peter had taken, all he had given Neal this night, release still eluded Neal. It was unbearable. Peter shuddered and heaved above him, hips pumping, firing, filling Neal's channel, a thousand pins of ecstasy torturing his body. He couldn't stop the single sob. It burst out under guise of a groan. He would never be happy, never free of the Judge's humiliation and abuse.

His cock twitched and bobbed, engorged with an impossible weight, a scorching need that seemed as helplessly restrained and bound as the ghost was in the cursed watch.

Warmth wrapped around his cock, fingers, long and callus, still and strong. Neal's face was turned toward the candle glow and held there. Peter stared down only far enough away that Neal could focus on his face, the sternness in the lines around his eyes, the gentleness of his gaze, understand the firmness of his confident tone when he demanded, "Mine. You. Are. Mine."

Lightning struck the room. Or Neal just imagined it had. His body seemed as if it exploded. His cock jerked, spurts of pearly droplets glistening in the light. As they landed, Peter swiped them into this palm to rub onto his chest, licking his fingers to get every last bit. He leaned in the last few inches and kissed Neal hard, sharing the taste of the younger man's release.

Neal moaned at the intimacy of the action, then pulled away, screaming.

The bedchamber door burst open. Hinges scattered, the dense wooden door flapped, swinging on broken wings. A cold wind whirled into the room, smoky clouds of black and gray, thinner, paler than before. It trembled, screeching in a reedy, frenzied call. It flowed through the room in an instant, long fingers grasping at Neal's still screaming lips, its gaping black hole of a mouth desperately trying to seal them together, to swallow down the anguished sounds.

Neal's skin crawled, a thousand insects scurried under

his flesh, as if feeding from a decaying corpse. His chest was raw, flames crisped the hairs across his heart, the air in his lungs searing, filled with suffocating fumes that reeked of sulfur and iron. Daggers lanced through his eyes, his scalp tightened, the screams torn from his throat were filled with pain, agony on his ears. He could see Peter trying to fight off the shadow, rolling Neal away, covering his body with his own, trying fiercely to shield him from the darkness.

But still it clawed at him, Clawed and clawed and clawed. Never gaining entrance but still on this side of the gates of hell. This would be the last thing he felt and heard. Not Peter, not the memory of their joining, not the joy he'd finally found. Agony and terror. Williams had won after all. The room faded. Neal knew he was on the verge of blacking out. He wanted his last sight to be of Peter, but his strength was spent. He closed his eyes, darkness preferable to the devil's tool pinning him down.

The darkness lifted. Neal could breathe again. His eyes fluttered open, lungs raw, the taste of evil still clung to his lips. Peter held on to him tightly, cursed oaths accompanying each swing of his fist at the shadowed form.

Ayana stood at the threshold of the chamber drawing ancient symbols from Williams' rituals in the air, her eerie singsong chant, rapid and strong, loud enough to be heard over the spirit's wailing screeches. She called to the demon, coaxed it to her, her amulet hung around her neck, the pouch strings open, the scent of spice and earth mixing with the smell of men and sex.

The ghost answered her. It reared up from the bed

and dove at her, weak, frenzied, almost transparent. As it approached Ayana met it head on, tossing dirt into its open mouth. Flames bellowed out of the fireplace, long talons that slashed the shadow into strips of gray smoke. The flames instantly died away, sucking the ribbons of darkness down with them. Stillness filled the room.

A weight lifted off Neal's chest. His head cleared, his body relaxed, the pain gone. Nothing was left behind but the vague sensation of anticipation.

"Thank you, Ayana. Peter..." Suddenly he realized he was in Peter's arms, naked, both of them, with nothing, not even linen between them and Ayana's gaze. Neal wasn't sure he had the energy to find a cover but Peter rose to the occasion, shielding Neal's lower half with a generous thigh. As grateful as he was, this was awkward.

"Ah, Ayana? Do you think you could give a moment of privacy?" Ayana averted her gaze but not as quickly as Neal would have liked. Instead of leaving the room she moved closer.

"I destroyed the watch." She tossed the mangled timepiece onto the bed. For the first time Neal noticed her dress was torn and hair cap missing. She blotted a trickle of blood from her lip with the edge of her apron. "No more shadows in your lifetime, child. Leave the darkness and secrets to others."

"Unfortunately, I don't think my life will be entirely free from the need for secrets, Ayana." He traced the ridge of Peter's broad cheek with a light touch, one that made the other man shiver and put a smile on his face. "I hope I get better at keeping them though."

"You'll have help. Lucky for you I'm excellent with secrets." Peter's voice was rough again, desire creeping back into his eyes.

"Even now?"

"Especially now. I told you, Neal. You're mine."

"You'll both have help." She turned and walked to the threshold, shoving the door upright. "Mister Clifton has sent you a gift to celebrate your...partnership. A housekeeper who can do the wash, cook and clean *and* keep a secret. I have no quarrel with your way of life, if you have no quarrel with mine."

"Ayana!" Pleased, both men rose part way off the bed but quickly dropped back down to preserve their dignity. Ayana laughed and left, the broken door swaying in her wake.

They shared a dazed look, Neal was amazed at how quickly Peter had adjusted to the events of the last two days, his strength, confidence and sense of right were unshakeable, even in the face of unearthly madness.

Peter twisted around and found the coverlet. He swept it up off the floor, tucking it around both of them. Neal grabbed the watch from the bedding to keep it from being lost. It was hopelessly bent, cold, but only the cold of ordinary metal, lifeless and silent.

"Should I keep it as a reminder?" Neal frowned, his mood darkening. "A cautionary tale of the error of letting desire rule reason?"

Plucking it from Neal's hand, Peter tossed it on the bedside table. "No. We don't need any reminders of this day."

Peter rolled to his back and took Neal with him, laying chest to chest, Peter's stiffening cock between his thighs. The look of need in Peter's eyes sent a thrill of pleasure down Neal's spine.

"Besides, Master Clifton, I intend to have a lifetime of you allowing desire to rule your reason. And mine."

About the Author

Laura Baumbach is the award-winning author of numerous short stories, novellas, novels and screenplays. Her favorite genre to work in is manlove or m/m erotic romances. Manlove is not traditional gay fiction, but erotic romances written specifically for the romantic-minded reader, male or female. Married to the same man for almost 30 years, she currently lives with her husband and two sons in the blustery Northeast of the United States but is looking for a warmer location to spend the second half of her professional and family life.

Laura is the owner of ManLoveRomance Press, founded in January of 2007. You can find Laura on the internet at:

http://www.laurabaumbach.com/

http://groups.yahoo.com/group/laurabaumbachfiction

http://www.mlrpress.com/

http://groups.yahoo.com/group/mlrpress/

www.ingramcontent.com/pod-product-compliance
Lightning Source LLC
Chambersburg PA
CBHW071257250626
47159CB00004B/1223